My Son

Is Out There

Somewhere

Carrie Arnold

authorHOUSE®

AuthorHouse™
1663 Liberty Drive
Bloomington, IN 47403
www.authorhouse.com
Phone: 1 (800) 839-8640

Published by AuthorHouse   02/18/2017

ISBN: 978-1-5246-6889-1 (sc)
ISBN: 978-1-5246-6888-4 (e)

Print information available on the last page.

This book is printed on acid-free paper.

Foreword

Cynthia Pate: White woman: Early Sixties:
Beautician

I loved this novel. It held my interest from the beginning to the end. If you had to put it down, you cannot wait to get back to it. I enjoyed the twists concerning the twins and especially the ending.

Eva Hansen: Black woman: Mid Seventies:
Retired Educator:

This novel is a page turner. It's a very good read that flows. It's almost like a mystery until the final chapter. I cried at the ending. I truly enjoyed it.

Stephen Reeves: Black man: Early Forties: Firefighter

This novel is very good. I thoroughly enjoyed it. The twists made it better than other novels of this nature. This should be a movie.

Dianne Watkins: White woman: Mid Sixties: Nurse

This novel is very hot. After reading it, I had to go back to my boyfriend. However, this novel is too short; I need more.

Roderick Parker: Black man: Mid Fifties: Massage Therapist

This novel is captivating. When I started reading it, I could not stop until I had finished. I feel that this could be an interesting movie.

Rosetta Richard: Black woman: Mid Sixties: Retired Employee Relations Rep. for Mississippi Power Company:

This novel captured my attention. I enjoyed it. It is a good read. The sex is explicit. I know others will enjoy it, as well.

Clara Craig: Black woman: Late Seventies: Retired US Postal Supervisor

This novel was easy to read and difficult to put down. It exhibits deceit, love and forgiveness with a surprising ending.

Mary Siaw: African woman: Mid Thirties: Nurse

I love this novel. It is suspenseful and keeps you reading until you finish it. I'm looking for a part two.

L. Kimbro: Black woman: Early Forties: Scheduling Coordinator & Motivational Speaker

This an exciting and suspenseful novel that holds your undivided attention from the beginning. It should be a Life Time movie.

Terrence L: Black man: Late Fifties: Professional Reader

I was spellbound reading this novel. I could not stop reading it until I finished it and I felt like I was there with the characters. There has to be a part two.

Roslyn L: Black woman: Late Sixties: Singer

This novel is a page turner with genuine love, unrequited love, sex, wealth, obsession, deception and spiritually with a dose of intrigue. An engaging replete that caused me to read on to see what the end would be.

Dollie Lynn: Black woman: Early Sixties: Retired Govt Employee

It is hard to put this novel down because it is a good read that holds your interest. It is well organized and flows well. Great ending; I loved how it wrapped up. I wish it were longer. I'm looking for the second one.

Aissatou Diallo: African woman: Early Thirties: Nurse

The novel is so easy to read and it causes you to think. I could not stop reading it. I had to find out what was next. Part of it felt like it was my story. I am anxious to read the second one. I know it is coming.

Peggy Spaulding: Black woman: Late Seventies: Entrepreneur

This novel was quite interesting. I was anxious to see how it would end. It kept my attention from the beginning through the end.

Richard Wade: Black man: Late Sixties: Retired Auditor/Analysis

This novel is an entertaining easy read and incorporates many aspects of life today; unfaithfulness, forgiveness, stalking and kidnapping. The mixture of the common place as well as the non-common place creates suspense making it difficult to put the book down until it is completely read.

Dorothy Kelly: Black woman: Mid Sixties: General Merchandise Retail Manager/ Retired Minority Health Consultant for the US Federal Government

This novel was brilliantly written. I was excited and curious to finish it. The story displayed power, excitement, deceit, bigotry, as well as love with a happy ending. I hope a second one is coming.

Miriam Lucier: Black woman: Mid Seventies: Retired Vocational Counselor

This novel is very good. I enjoyed it from the beginning. I am sitting on the edge of my seat waiting for the second one. This would make a very good movie.

Ann Byars: Black woman: Late Sixties: Ex Nurse (LPN) / Retired Sale Rep (Delta Air Lines)

This novel is an easy read that I thoroughly enjoyed. Because of the twists in the story, I could not stop reading it until I had completely finished it. The ending was quite a surprise. I hope there is a sequel.

Edna James: Black woman: Early Sixties: Retired Financial Manager:

This novel is an easy read. I really enjoyed the story because it held my attention.

Beverly Newton: Black woman: Late Fifties: (IT) Support

The plot was interesting; I love the story line. I liked the emphasis on forgiveness and family.

Flu Dugger: Black woman: Late Sixties: Hair Stylist

I loved reading this novel. This was an easy read that I could not stop reading until I finished it. I feel that this should be considered for a movie.

Ezora Grundy: Black woman: Late Fifties: Wife/ Mother/ Government Worker

I really enjoyed this novel. This is truly a good story about God's love and forgiveness at work. It is also a true testament to the power of prayer. I loved reading about the children's enthusiasm of being together and their pure hearts toward one another.

Ann-Marie Craig: White woman: Early Forties: Homemaker/Wife/Mother

The plot is great. The novel is indepth, intense and wound together. Angelica had no regard for anyone, except herself.

Kathy Bryant: Black woman: Early Fifties: Corporate Tax Accountant

This novel is a wonderful, captivating quick read. It covers many family issues.

Charlotte Haliburton: Black woman: Late Sixties: Retired Design Assistant for Bell South

The novel is an easy read that is very entertaining. It's like a mystery. It keeps you wondering where the story is going next. I was pleased with the ending.

June Faizi: White woman: Mid Seventies: Retired: Grants Management Specialist for the Federal Government

I really enjoyed this novel. I particular liked the unexpected twist at the end.

Adrienne Randolph: Black woman: Early Twenties: Student

This novel is an easy read. I enjoyed it.

William Moore: Black man: Early Forties: Entrepreneur

I enjoyed the novel (the story and the plot). It was an easy read and I am looking forward to the sequel. The ending makes me believe one is coming.

Thomas Redding: Black man: Late Sixties: Retired Military Veteran/ Educator/ Minister

This novel is entertaining, intriguing and also shocking, sad and insulting, but indulging and engaging at the same time. When I started reading it, I could not stop until I finished it.

Sheila Young: Black woman: Early Sixties: Retired US Postal Manager

This novel has a great plot with unexpected twists!! It leaves you yearning for more. It could easily be transformed into a movie. I can't wait for the sequel to follow up on the twins.

Myrtice Hampton:

I enjoyed this novel. It is awesome. I like the contents and the ease of reading. It is an exciting, sensitive and powerful story. I kept reading to see where the next turn was taking me. I could not put it down until I had finished reading it.

Rozzie Youngblood: Black woman: Late Sixties: Retired Nurse/Minister/Care Giver/Cook

This is an easy read, wonderful novel. It held my attention; I was hooked. I could not stop reading until I had finished it.

Nancy Henry: Black woman: Early Sixties: Retired Nurse

I enjoyed this novel. It was really a delightful page turner. I was anxious to see what would happen next.

Joann Chandler: Black woman: Early Fifties:

This novel is something else. I enjoyed reading it. I could not stop reading until I finished it. Angelica was a piece of work. It was great reading; I loved it.

Vickie James, MD: Black woman: Early Fifties: Family Practitioner

I truly enjoyed reading this novel. It is a page turner that holds your attention from the beginning to the end. It is suspenseful with a very good surprising ending. Maybe this would make an entertaining movie.

Carolyn Davenport: Black woman: Mid Sixties: Ex-Flight Attendant / Retired Educator

This novel is a very interesting, suspenseful good read. It touches on reality. The love making scenes also adds to the reader's attention. I hope there is a sequel. This story might make an interesting play, movie or motion picture.

James Pittman: Black man: Early Sixties: Retired Communications Technician

This novel is an easy read. I did not stop reading until I had finished it. The story first included trickery and deceit then brought in love and forgiveness.

Terrence Arnold: Black man: Mid Fifties: Care Giver

When I read this novel, I was surprised at how good it really is. The words that came to mind were powerful and emotional, causing me to cry at least twice. Although it is an easy read, it is captivating. It holds your attention from beginning to end. Then you want more. . There must be a sequel.

Gail Stinchfield: White woman: Early Sixties: Retired Govt. Employee

This novel is intriguing. I can't wait for the sequel. Since Angelica always gets what she wants, I must know if she ever gets the man she continues to want.

James Smith: Black man: Early Sixties: Ex-Soldier / Retired

This novel is good like a delicious meal that you just ate, knowing you shouldn't lick your fingers, but you do anyway. I am expecting a sequel.

Lucy Chandler: Black woman: Late Sixties: Retired US Postal Worker

I enjoyed this novel. It is an easy read with lots of interesting twists. I am looking for the second one.

Dolores Watkins: Black woman: Mid Sixties: Retired Govt. Employee- Minister

This novel depicts how life challenges you and take you on unexpected and unanticipated journeys to end at an unforeseen place. Maybe there will be a sequel aspiring to more life situations. I hope there is.

Laura Stone: Hispanic woman: Late Seventies: Retired Government Employee

This novel is very interesting. I did not stop reading until I had finished it. I liked the surprise ending. This should be a play or a movie.

Sergio Adame: Hispanic man:
Late Fifties: Law Enforcement

This novel is good. I enjoyed it and I read it from beginning to the end. The ending was a pleasant surprise.

Preface

I was incapacitated for more than ten days. Whenever I moved around, the arthritis pain that I suffered was almost unbearable. I could not cook, clean or do things that required movement. If I sat up or laid in bed, I was ok; almost pain free. Nevertheless, I was developing cloister phobia and cabin fever from having to stay inside for so long.

I had to do something to keep from going "stir crazy". Since I enjoy writing, I decided to go to my computer and write something. I thought I would write poems, but the idea of a novel came to mind. "My Son Is Out There Somewhere" is the manuscript that was born from my keeping myself from being bored to tears.

Acknowledgments

I will always remember and appreciate my deceased supervisor, John E. Awalt. He was the first person to tell me that I should try my hand at writing. After seeing some of the poems I had written, he told me that I should try writing more poems, plays or maybe even books.

I would like to thank my cousin, Carolyn Davenport for suggesting that I write something, every day since I had retired.

I want to thank my loving husband, Terrence Arnold for also encouraging me write after I retired. He read whatever I wrote and discussed its contents with me. This was so helpful.

I am also appreciative of my friend, James R. Smith for taking time out of his busy schedule to allow me to read to him, my novel (My Son Is Out There Somewhere). James gave me very positive feedback and encouragement.

I really appreciate my many friends who took the time to read my manuscript (My Son Is Out There Somewhere) and gave me their honest feedback. With their permission, I have included each of them in the Foreward. I thank all of you so much!!

Introduction

This novel was written to be a suspenseful, intriguing, exciting, interesting manuscript. It is supposed to be an easy read that holds the reader's attention. The twists in it are to keep the reader wanting to continue to see where the novel will take them next. I thought the ending might be a bit of a surprise.

I hope that this novel will be a discussion piece by its readers in many places, in many walks of life.

List of Contributors

My devoted niece, Sheila S. Young was the person that I could depend on for advice, concern and/or correction in writing this novel. She was positive, encouraging and helpful in assisting me in formatting the entire book. Every time I talked with Sheila, she asked, "How is the novel coming?" She was always ready to listen and help me make decisions, even on whether or not to get the work published. I was thinking of self- publishing, but Sheila talked me out of that. Sheila and Leslie Kimbro, another dear friend are the reason that I published with Author House.

MY SON IS OUT THERE SOMEWHERE

Leonard and Catherine Parker were among the wealthiest oil tycoons in the State of Texas (estimated worth 5.3 billion dollars). Since neither of them had siblings, they wanted to have as many children as possible. But as fate had it, they only had one; Angelica Lorraine. Although Angelica was not a ravishing beauty with a prim and proper, but sexy walk like her mother, she had an attractive face and a nice smile. But Angelica grew up to be 5' 4" tall with reddish brown, thick long flowing hair and an extremely shapely body and beautiful legs like her mother. Angelica was lovely inside and out, both physically and emotionally. She was always happy and loved and trusted everyone so her parents protected her from everything and everyone that might cause her harm. Her parents also gave her everything she needed and wanted and many unnecessary things that they just wanted her to have. This made Angelica extremely spoiled, thinking she could have whatever she wanted; when she wanted it, no matter what the cost. Angelica had a glowing personality, but her parents never told her that you can't always get what you want when you want it. Sometimes you get what you get when you get it. Angelica had no experience in getting what she got when she got it, because she had always gotten what she wanted when she wanted it.

However, Angelica was more advanced than most children her age because she was home schooled by her mother and was exposed to many diverse things through her world-wide travel experiences with her parents. Her parents were so protective of her, Angelica never learned the mechanics of how to protect herself from people who might try to hurt or misuse her. Angelica also believed whatever anyone told her, simply because that was what they said. Her parents never allowed her to visit or sleep over at other children's homes. However, Angelica did enjoy socializing at birthday parties, holiday events, cook outs and other celebrations at other people's exquisite homes and sometimes at elaborate venues in town and out of town, as well. When she attended these events, her sometimes acquaintances there were the children of her parents' friends, business partners, associates and on very rare occasions, some of her parents mere acquaintances.

Because of Angelica's extremely high tests scores and her perfect 1,600 SAT score, at the early age of 16, she went off to college where she met Jonathan Gamble, one of the most handsome, intelligent debonair men at Yale University. Jonathan became anxious to date Angelica when he learned that her father was a billionaire.

Jonathan knew that Angelica wanted to date him, too by the way she looked at him with a childish grin on her face every time she saw him so he took his time asking her for a date. For a long time, since Jonathan was already involved with three other women, he simply greeted Angelica with, "Hello PYT, Pretty Young Thing," while winking his eye at her as he slowly walked pass her. Jonathan was a graduate student already. In four more years he would obtain his second Master's and a PhD. Because he was slow to ask her for a date and since Angelica was accustomed to getting what she wanted when she wanted it, she started dating some of her other suitors, including one of her college professors who she lost her virginity to, as well as the son of one of her father's business associates. But none of these relationships meant much to her because Angelica was still obsessed with having what she wanted. She continued to want Jonathan Gamble. Finally, after two years, Jonathan asked her out and they started dating only once or twice a week because he continued to date other women without Angelica knowing. But of course, she trusted that he loved her and wanted her only, because that was what he told her. Even after she graduated from college, she still trusted anything anyone told her, especially Jonathan.

Her father, Leonard Parker did not believe that Jonathan loved his daughter as much as he wanted the man in Angelica's life to love her. Even though Jonathan had two undergraduate degrees, one in Accounting and one in Business Administration with a specialty in Human Resources; two Master's, one in Business Administration with a concentration in Project Management and one in Business Law; and a PhD in Management with a concentration in

Organizational Behavior, Jonathan could/would probably always be gainfully employed, but he was not likely to become the kind of rich man Leonard Parker wanted for his precious daughter. However, after dating for two and a half years, when they graduated, the two told Angelica's parents they wanted to get married. Angelica parents realized that she wanted so much to be married to Jonathan, they very reluctantly approved and Angelica, Jonathan and Angelica's parents began making wedding plans.

However, prior to the wedding, Leonard Parker made it quite clear, both verbally and in writing in a notarized document to Jonathan Gamble that his name would not be attached to any portion of the Parker's wealth until his precious daughter had been happily married to him for ten years and at least one child had been birth into that union.

When the expenditures for the wedding were compiled, the total cost was astounding. However, the exorbitant cost for this most beautiful 5.8 million dollar wedding was of no concern to Angelica's father since her happiness was Leonard Parker's main concern. Renting the Chateau Carnarvon, the most fabulous and most expensive real estate venue in Houston from one of his friends from Thursday morning through Sunday night was one of the gift's Mr. Parker gave his precious baby girl (the pet name he called Angelica). He had his chest stuck out and a very slight smile on his face the entire time because his daughter was so happy with all of the arrangements leading up to her outstanding wedding with her pride and joy; the love of her life, Jonathan Gamble.

The weather could not have been more beautiful the weekend of September 25 through September 28, 1990. The warm sun shinny temperatures ranged from 78 to 87 degrees all weekend for the guests who chose to come early on Thursday or Friday and stay thru Sunday night to enjoy the many activities and the varying amenities at Leonard Parker's friend's breath taking venue. As they say, "everybody who was anybody" was there.

The more than 1,500 guests were comprised mostly of the wealthy, the rich, very rich, the filthy rich, many dignitaries (some from other countries), a few upper and middle class people, all of the Parker's and Gamble's families, friends, neighbors, business partners and associates and many families and friends of the bridal party and their employees, who weren't servicing the wedding. Almost all nations and races were there to witness this beautiful, elaborate, memorable extravaganza in the exchange of the marriage vows between Angelica Parker and Jonathan Gamble. And everyone who could stay the entire time – **Did.** They stayed to partake in the planned and the impromptu events at this breathtaking place. Every day and night, the guests were introduced to new people, as they drank, danced, laughed, swam, made jokes and even sang together and competed in games for fun, as if they were all old friends of many, many years who had not seen each other for a long while. As it is often stated, "Everybody partied hardy".

Sunday, after the beautiful, exquisite wedding and everything else was over, although everyone remained excited and happy, they were all so very tired and ready to go home. Angelica and Jonathan were so exhausted, they had to stay at Chateau Carnarvon until Monday evening before they could even think about moving themselves or overseeing the moving of their many, many gifts and other belongings to their very lovely, new home in Minnesota.

The fabulous wedding and their lovely house on five acres of land were the wedding gifts from Angelica's parents, Leonard and Catherine Parker. Their gifts from Jonathan's parents were the couple's two week honeymoon in Las Vegas and two new automobiles (a Ferrari for Jonathan and a Bentley for Angelica) which were parked in the garage at their new home with the keys inside the automobiles that Angelica and Jonathan would not get to see until after their two week honeymoon in Vegas. Their all-expense paid honeymoon was off the chain, too. They must have been the happiest couple alive when they finally went to their new home where the automobiles of their dreams awaited them. Jonathan carried his bride over the threshold and into their master bedroom on the main floor for some much needed sleep, rest and recuperation. For three days they only woke up to have sex, eat and bathe. But my, were they in love and happy.

Three months before their wedding, Jonathan had chosen to live in Minnesota because he thought that might be far enough away from Angelica's parents, particularly his father-in-law, Leonard Parker. Therefore, he convinced Angelica that relocating there would be ideal because he had accepted a job as an Executive Director of an extremely large, luxurious 900 bed Health Care Facility for the wealthy in Minnesota. Angelica told her father the cost of the property and that Minnesota was where she wanted to live, so Mr. Parker wrote the check for them to purchase the lovely new six bedroom, five and a half bath property in her name.

Although Jonathan's $450,000.00 annual salary was nothing like the kind of income Angelica's father earned, it was adequate to maintain the kind of lifestyle she was used to, since they had no car or mortgage payments. Jonathan salary was more than enough to pay their monthly expenses, sponsor their vacations, maintain their luxury automobiles and for their many trips to visit relatives and friends, attend plays and other events, to buy Angelica extravagant gifts for their many nights out and out-of-town, out-of-the-country entertainment as well as money to deposit into their handsome savings and investment accounts.

Angelica didn't concern herself with Jonathan's salary, because she had a $39,000 monthly dividends check from a $5,000,000.00 investment her father had made for her before she turned sixteen and went off to college. She'd been depositing most of her interest checks into an off-shore account since she started receiving them over seven years ago. Angelica was a rich woman without her father's money. Although Jonathan did not know about Angelica's personal finances, he knew she could get whatever money she wanted from her father but he would never have asked her for money because he knew if her father ever got wind of something like that, Mr. Parker would lose the little respect that he had for him and would never add his name to any part of the Parker's wealth.

For the first three and a half years of marriage, Mrs. Angelica Parker/Gamble was very happy with her husband, Jonathan. She never questioned why he worked late so often or why his job entailed so much travel. Jonathan habitually presented his sweet, loving wife very nice gifts even though sometimes, the size of some gifts were wrong (too small). But Angelica thought nothing of this until one day a large, padded, sealed envelope fell out of the back of one of Jonathan closets, behind some of his old suits that she had planned to give to a charity that picked up unwanted items. Angelica got scissors and tore into the wrapped package which contained receipts dating back two to three years for flowers and expensive gifts that she had not yet received. She notified the Bank shown on the receipts to apprise them of the errors they had made on the many charges to her husband's bank debit card with their Bank. The bank executive was in awe. She apologized, assuring Mrs. Gamble that she would check to see what in the world could have happened in this many incidents, over such a long period of time. After checking the records, the bank executive called and guaranteed Mrs. Gamble that the funds for all of the purchases were deducted from Mr. Gamble's bank debit card on the dates he requested and sent to the merchants for delivery to 4440 Jacobs Drive here in Minnesota. Each merchant had records to validate that all deliveries were made and none were returned.

It's a good thing that Jonathan was out of the Country in India because Angelica would have called to tell him about the receipts she had found. You see, her husband, Jonathan had told her that he could only be contacted on his cell phone between five thirty and seven o'clock each evening when his hard working group took a break before reconvening until eleven or twelve o'clock at night when he would be too exhausted to think, concentrate, let alone -- talk. Every morning about 9:00 AM, Jonathan called Angelica to say, "Hi Sweetheart; hope you slept good because I hardly slept at all; I am so tired but I must run now; I'm running late, as usual; I love you; see you soon" then hanging up without giving Angelica a chance to tell him anything that had happened at home. When he returned home from his business trips, they were to make love, lay in each other's arms and just sleep, relax and chill-out, hardly saying anything to each other. She would lay there watching him sleep for many hours, because she knew she had to wait until he had been home a day or two before they could discuss anything of importance, you know—anything that might be stressful. You see, whenever he came home, he was always too tired to deal with anything that required serious thinking.

Since Jonathan would not return for three more weeks and Angelica's curiosity had gotten the best of her, she decided to have their driver take her to 4440 Jacobs Drive. She reluctantly got out of the car, walked to the door at this very lovely, dimly lighted house and slowly rang the doorbell that chimed the song, "Love, Love Will Keep Us Together". A very thin, but shapely beautiful young woman answered the door and said, "Hello, whose guest are you?" Angelica did not know what to say, but she could see through the crack in the slightly opened door that there was an exhilarating party going on inside with maybe twenty to thirty people. "Oh, I just wanted to know who lives at this address." The woman said, "I do". "Hello, my name is Charlie Chastaine." Still smiling, she said "who are you and what can I do for you". Angelica said, "I am Angelica Gamble". "An executive at National Bank of Minnesota said that for the last two to three years or more charges from my husband's bank debit card for flowers and many other gifts were delivered to this address from him, Jonathan Gamble". "Do you know him"? At this point, Charlie Chastaine began to scream, seems like as loud as she could, **"What? Yes I Know Him. Are You Saying That You Are Jonathan Gamble's Wife?** But before Angelica could answer, Charlie continued, **"That Lying Asshole; That Conniving Son Of A Bitch. He Always Told Me That He Wasn't Married". This Is One Lie That He'll Be Sorry That He Told.** At this, with tears running down her cheeks, Angelica ran as fast as she could back to the car, swiftly jumped in, told the driver to take her home as fast as he could. Charlie could not contact Jonathan because he was already on a flight, in route to her house. As soon as Charlie saw Jonathan pull up, she ran outside to his car, flung the car door open and when she laid eyes on him she said, in the same very loud voice, **"You Filthy, Low Down, Lying, Deceitful Son Of A Bitch". "You Swore That You Were NOT Married". "You Had Me Thinking That We Would Get Married As Soon As You Straightened Out Some Unfinished Business With A Family Member," "I Hate You". "I'm Going To Sue Your Damn Pants Off; You Stupid Asshole". "You Will Hear From My Attorney, Tomorrow".** Before Jonathan could say a word, Charlie slammed his car door and ran back into her house and without looking at her guests, she shouted, **"This Party Is Over; All Of you, Get Out, Now."** Then she ran into to her bedroom and threw herself on the bed and cried uncontrollably for hours.

While thinking of what to say to Angelica, Jonathan drove very slowly and when he got home, he went into the downstairs bedroom where he saw his swollen eyed wife, Angelica sitting quietly on the side of the bed, with the lamp light on dim. He still didn't know what to do or say, but he knew that he had to somehow make it right with her. After all, she was his Extravagant Meal Ticket - His Future - His More Lavish Lifestyle. He began to reach for her while saying, "Honey, baby, my lovely, wonderful wife, please don't believe anything that that Charlie woman said". "She's just jealous and she's trying to break us up. "She does not mean anything to me". "Please believe me". "I love you, only". With the look of hurt all over her face Angelica looked up at him but she said nothing. She could not speak. When she was able to speak she said, "Because of your secret account with all of those purchases on your bank debit card there, "I know that you had an affair with Charlie Chastaine. Jonathan said, "Angelica, my love, as he begged and began to cry himself. "You're right I am so sorry. I don't know why I did such a terrible thing to you; to our beautiful marriage please, please forgive me. This is the biggest mistake that I have ever made." "But I promise that from this day forward, I will never be unfaithful to you again." Still crying, he reached for and touched her hand. He knelt in front of her and cried more and more.

Jonathan cried and begged and begged and cried so convincingly, Angelica forgave him with the condition that he would never have another affair, ever again. But before she told him that she forgave him, she told him, "As we both already know, "my father will have you killed if I tell him what you did". "I know, I Know", Jonathan said, as he hugged and thanked her profusely, "Thank, you, thank you, thank you, you won't regret this". From now on, I will always be good to you and true to you". She would not let him kiss her, but he held onto her hand for hours until they fell asleep.

It took Angelica quite a while before she could let Jonathan kiss her or touch her in that special way. He assigned much of his work that entailed traveling to other employees and things slowly got back to normal. Whenever Angelica saw her father or talked with him on the phone, she pretended that Jonathan was the greatest husband any woman could have.

In several months, when Jonathan started traveling again, he got back into his old habits. The woman he dated this time lived out of State so he could spend lots of time with her when he was in or near the town where she lived and/or worked. When he dated others, he even became brave enough to have them meet him in or near his designated work areas out of town. He ended most of his relationships after a few weeks but he stayed in one or two of them for two or three months. In a fourteen month period, he may have had ten to twelve extra marital affairs because in about ten months he started dating more than one woman at a time for short periods.

But back at home, after pondering over and over again, the Charlie Chastaine incident, Angelica realized Jonathan had no reason to be unfaithful to her and this had done much damage to her trust in him. As a matter of fact, Angelica never again believed what someone said simply because they said it. She remained so suspicious of Jonathan, she hired a private detective who informed her of each new mistress and she kept tabs on his purchases: (what purchased, when and at what price) She was never again in the dark after his first affair. Because Angelica was duly informed, her love for Jonathan diminished with each of his affairs. Her heart was finally hardened toward him. She could hardly stand the sight of him. Although Jonathan was an extremely unfaithful man, somewhere along the way, his desire to have Angelica had grown and grown. She was the only woman that he truly wanted.

Although Angelica was very unhappy, and suffered in silence but she remained faithful to Jonathan and never looked at another man – until one day......!!

Their 5+ acre property was maintained by Manicured to Perfection Lawn Care Service. Every week five men from that business, using all the latest lawn care equipment kept the curb appeal of their home so immaculate, it had heads turning and fingers pointing when people passed by, while saying, "Oh wow, look at that. How beautiful!"

One day several of the employees of Manicured to Perfection became ill from the flu virus. On the day that the Gamble's lawn was to be serviced; the owner of the company, Terrence Watson had to do the work himself. Even though Terrence worked with precision as he always did, he knew it would take him at least three days to complete the work of the five men. However, on the first day, Angelica looked out of the side of the drapery at the front window and was shocked at this masterpiece of a 6' 5" curly haired man in a wet, white tee shirt that clung to his body. His arms had big hard, bulging muscles that needed to be felt by her; a six pack that she felt herself wanting to rub and a very hard looking chest that she could see herself lying on. She could also envision his long, strong, slightly bowed legs around her hips. His lips looked so kissable. He needed her to kiss his lips, then burn with her in desire. "Oh my, God, **what in the world is happening to me?**" "I have never felt like this before". She could not stop staring at him. He had so many sexy attributes that she hadn't even noticed that he was a **black** man. All she knew was she really wanted to touch him and be touched by him, **ALL OVER.** Her mouth was open and she hadn't realized that she had moved over and was now standing in his clear view, in front of the window. When he looked up, she slowly raised her right hand and waved at him and she let her left hand just limply hanging down by her left hip. She felt strange, extremely limp and almost helpless. **She had truly been through something that she didn't understand just from watching him through her front window.** After he saw her wave at him, he smiled and waved back and walked to the front steps and onto the porch. She slowly opened the door and saw his ripped body up close and heard his a very deep, base, sexy voice say, "Hi, I didn't think anyone was home. My name is Terrence Watson from Manicured to Perfection Lawn Care Service and I am here to take care of your lawn. I'll be working alone so it'll probably take me at least three days to finish. If that is OK with you and your husband". She said in a very low, hoarse, raspy voice, as she reached to shake his hand, "Oh that will be fine, I'm Angelica Gamble. Take as long as you need". When she saw her pale hand in his brown one, Angelica realized Terrence Watson was black, but she did not care because she wanted him even more. After seeing how tall and robust he really was, she wanted so much to touch him. Then Angelica said something that surprised her, "My husband won't be home for two more weeks". Then she thought, "What the hell; I want to see this man; I want to; heck, I want to touch him; I want him to touch me". Then she thought, "my God, Help me". "Yes, God, please help me." Help me to get this man." "You have always given me whatever I want, so please God give this Terrence Watson to me."

Terrence gently released her hand and said, "Well, Mrs. Gamble, I'd better get back to work now", and he did. Angelica could not stay away from the window, whichever one was near where he was working. That night, she could not sleep and did not care that her husband did not call. As a matter of fact, she was glad that the phone did not ring. All night she thought and thought of ways to get this Terrence Watson. How could she ask him to meet her somewhere -- anywhere? All she knew was that she **had** to devise some way to get to him. The next day, Angelica rushed to the front door when she saw Terrence Watson driving his truck onto their property with all of his lawn equipment attached. She opened the front door and beckoned for him to come in. When he reached for the door knob, she flung the door opened, then Terrence said, "Yes, Mrs. Gamble, what can I do for you"? "Great question!!" "You can do a lot for me, Terrence." Angelica said, with what Terrence thought was a lustful look in her eyes. At this, Terrence began to feel outrageously uncomfortable and strange. She stepped forward with her hand outreached to touch him. He instantly stepped back and said, "Mrs. Gamble", in a very heavy, stern voice, "you are a married woman and I am engaged to my fiancée, Sheila Smith, the woman that I truly love with all of my heart." She thought to herself, "I don't care", but instead she said, "Oh, I am so sorry". "I am sorry that you are not interested in becoming my friend because I think I would love to be yours. Well I guess, I am sorry for myself because, although we have lived here for years, I have no friends and my husband's job requires lots of traveling. I would love to have someone to just converse with, sometimes. You see, I don't trust most people, but I feel something when I see you that I have never felt before".

Terrence turned and reached for the door. When Angelica said, "Please don't go. Let's talk". Terrence said, "I don't see what we could have to talk about". "Until you sit down and listen, you won't know what I want to talk about with you." With this, Terrence sat in the chair closest to the door and said, "What is it?" "Why is it so necessary for us to talk?" "You see," said Angelica, "You are the first person that I just know in my spirit is an intelligent, honest, trustworthy, businessman that I feel that I can accept as a friend. I have never met anyone that I have sensed this much about in my life. I just know that you are the kind of person that I can be honest and converse with sometimes; a distant friend of a sort". I know your company has taken care of our grounds for years; ever since we moved here. And after meeting you yesterday, you seem so gentlemanly, calm and sure of yourself, I would like to develop a friendship with you if, at all possible. " Terrence said, "I'm sorry, I misunderstood your intentions; I thought you were trying to touch me in an inappropriate way". "I should have known better". "I'm sorry for the misunderstanding". She said, "Oh, that's okay", as she cleared her throat and regained her composure." "Well, with my busy schedule, I don't have lots of time, but I guess a new friend can be added if you're not requiring too much time," Terrence said. They gave each other a smile of agreement before he went out to start his day. Any day, after he had completed his tour of duty, whenever she called him, if he had time, he talked with her. He found that talking with her was somewhat enjoyable since she was so knowledgeable about so many things. But when he did not have time to talk, he told her. She was always polite and respected his time constraints. He began to like her and they became friends of a sort. Every now and again, they met for coffee, tea or a light lunch on his break when she happened to be near where he was working. It never dawned on him that she had paid a spy in his company to divulge his work week schedule so she would know where she could accidently run into him most weeks.

Before Terrence started talking with Angelica, he told his beloved Sheila about, maybe developing a friendship with a lonely woman whose lawn his company manicured. Sheila approved because she thought it was a good idea. Although Terrence had never had many friends, Sheila knew that he would make a good friend and probably be able to help this lonely person because he was such a good listener and could offer such profound advice if she needed it. Besides, Sheila had a close lifetime male friend that she enjoyed talking to and sometimes spending time with over coffee, tea or a light lunch. She had no insecurities, she knew that all of the important, personal things would always be discussed, shared and treasured with her and Terrence together. It never entered her mind that this lonely woman might have ulterior motives, **but she absolutely did**. You see, Angelica had never banished the thought of becoming intimate with and possessing Sheila's man; even **completely taking him** from Sheila someday—somehow. Angelica realized that

Terrence loved Sheila in a way that she wanted him to love her; with all of his heart, so she was waiting until the time was right; when she could make her move. She felt that she had to devise a way to get Sheila out of the picture. But, how? Angelica thought and thought and thought, many times all day and on occasions, all night.

Almost a year had passed and Angelica and Terrence had become friends, touching bases monthly or sometimes biweekly. "Hello, is everything OK with you? How's your family? What have you been doing? What did you think of the information in the newspaper article that I sent to you the other day? How is your husband or how is your fiancée?" is basically how the conversations went. And the answers were usually positive. On the few occasions, when the answers were negative or needed more discussion, Angelica would ask Terrence for an audience with him over coffee, tea or lunch. These conversations were more personal, often about her husband's infidelity and disrespect.

Terrence always listened intently and his answer, when asked, was always, "you deserve better". Angelica's response was usually, "I know, I know but letting go is so hard", until this particular day, when she said, "Terrence, the truth is that I am so afraid that my father will do something drastic to Jonathan, maybe even have him killed for mistreating and being unfaithful to his only daughter". Terrence said in a shocked voice, "Are you serious?" She forcefully said, "Absolutely serious." "I guess you don't know what a fool Leonard Parker is over **his baby girl** – the name he calls me". And yes, he already told Jonathan that if he finds out that he has done anything wrong to me, "that will be his ass". My father only curses when he is extremely upset and whatever he says, he will definitely do. You see, Terrence, my father does not tease." He also made it clear to Jonathan that he would not be included in any of the Parker's business nor the family's money until Jonathan has kept me happy for ten years and at least one child is birth into this union." Terrence said, "Wow the magnitude of this problem is more than any I had imagined". "Gosh, I am so sorry, I'm sure you feel stuck". "But you can't just stay in a relationship where you are being mistreated and disrespected like this". Angelica said, "Well, all I know is, I could never get over being the reason that my father had someone that I used to care about, **killed**". "Terrence, I just don't know what to do because I also don't want Jonathan's name to be put on the wealth that has been in my father's family for generations. "Well, Angelica, you must be much more patient. I am sure that an answer will surface". "Pray and God will let you know what to do, probably before the ten year period is over." "Are you alright?" She said, I'm better, knowing that I have shared this with you". "Good, I am glad that you are better, but I have no idea what I can do, except also pray for you and this situation and I definitely will." "Thank you, Terrence". They hugged and he said, "I must go back to work now but I will check on you, every day. Boy, was that good news to Angelica, "he'll check on me, Everyday". He did and talking with him every day made her so very happy. She waited everyday with anticipation because she yearned to hear his heavy, base, sexy voice. This made her feel even more things for him that she had never felt before. She knew that this everyday concern from him was what she had to have. She could never go back to talking to him every two weeks or once a month, as before.

All the while, Sheila's parents had always approved overwhelmingly of Sheila's choice of Terrence as her husband; and likewise, Terrence's parents equally approved of Sheila as Terrence's choice as his wife. You see, their parents had been friends since Sheila was only six years old when Terrence first started walking her to school Monday thru Friday and their families attended the same Church on Sundays. Therefore when Terrence and Sheila planned a get-away trip to decide on the best date to get married, they invited their parents along.

When Terrence called Angelica to let her know that for the next four or five days, she would not hear from him because he, Sheila and their parents were going on a three and a half day trip to decide on the best date for them to finally get married. The news infuriated Angelica; she became very angry and distraught; she slammed the phone down, then snatched off her shoes and threw them across the room, before she began to cry and she cried and cried and cried. All of a sudden, she stopped crying and thought, "What can I do to rectify this situation; how can I stop this woman from marrying *my man*"? She pondered over idea after idea trying to come up with the perfect plan that could work for her to get and keep Terrence, the man that obviously was supposed to belong to her.

Angelica was so busy thinking about Terrence and his impending marriage to Sheila Smith, she no longer cared when or where Jonathan was gone nor with whom nor for how long he was with whomever.

When Jonathan noticed Angelica's indifference, he started to concern himself more and more with his wife's feelings for him and their marriage. Actually, Jonathan realized he really needed this woman who had always loved him. He wanted and needed her to want him again; wanted her to make love to him the way she used to. Jonathan completely stopped having affairs with other women; he deferred his travel business to his subordinates as often as he could; he stopped drinking so much and started going home every day after he left his office. But most of the time when he got home from work, Angelica was not there. She came home late every night, around 11:00 or 12:00 or later. She told Jonathan she had been out with or had taken trips with friends he had never heard of. Sometimes, when he came home, she had left notes saying she had gone to visit friends or relatives and would be very late coming home, so don't wait up. Sometimes the note said she would be gone for a few days or a week or two. Actually, most days Angelica left home around 2:00 PM while Jonathan was at work and she went to a secluded place to be alone to create and develop the best plan to get rid of Sheila Smith. On a few occasions, Angelica stayed at a hotel in town for a week or two to allow herself enough time to put the right plan in place. She did not want to make any mistakes; she didn't want Sheila to reappear or come back to Terrence. Her plan had to be error proof.

At home, every now and again, maybe once every two or three months, Jonathan could devise a way to coerce Angelica into a sexual encounter with him. But she never seemed to enjoy him and only rushed him to finish, before turning her back and falling asleep. Jonathan was so lost and frustrated and hated the day he ever deceived and hurt her with his many senseless extra-marital affairs.

Meanwhile, the trip to the mountains with Terrence, Sheila and their parents went very well. They all agreed that Valentine's Day, February 14, 1994, which was less than thirty eight days away, would be the perfect date for Sheila and Terrence to be joined in holy matrimony.

Because Terrence and Sheila wanted no frills

and both had small families and very few friends, they decided to keep everything simple; they would be married by a Justice of the Peace at the Courthouse on Valentine's Day. Afterwards, they would have a small reception at Sheila's parents house with family members and their few friends. Then, aha, the next day, they would begin their two weeks honeymoon in Paris, France, the city of romance, where they would plan and discuss the details of the rest of their lives together, which was what really excited them most.

Meanwhile, Angelica spent most of her wake hours thinking about Terrence and awaiting his call when he returned from the trip with Sheila and their parents. By this time, Jonathan realized it was not the Parkers' prestige, money or fame. He really loved Angelica and wanted to save their marriage. Even though Jonathan had not a clue as to how to handle this situation, he had made a decision to do whatever it took to keep his wife and save his marriage.

Meantime, the next day after Terrence returned and told Angelica that he, Sheila and their parents had chosen February 14, 1994 as their date to be married.

Angelica had already decided what had to be

done to stop this impending marriage from taking place, "Sheila had to vanish!!" "If Sheila were to disappear and Terrence could never, ever find her, he would someday forget Sheila; get over her and then focus his attention, love and devotion on me." So Angelica got busy making sure that her scheme was flawless. She went over every detail, step by step, making sure no mistakes would be made. Her entire plan had to be error proof.

But almost a week after their returned from the trip Sheila began having these overwhelming, strange feelings that she needed to spend as much time with Terrence as possible. Sheila often insisted on being with Terrence at every waken moment – When they left work, she wanted him to shower and change clothes at her house. In the mornings, she wanted him to shower, shave and dress for work at her place. Terrence, realizing this was such unusual behavior from Sheila, ask her, "Baby, are you afraid that something might go wrong before we get married?" She said, "I don't know what's wrong with me, but I have the most bizarre feeling in my spirit". "It's as though, you will go away from me." Sheila, "I know that you know that you are the only woman that I want or will ever want for the rest of my life." "Yes, she said, but I can't shake these weird, scary feelings." "Well, it's OK baby." Every Friday after work, I'll bring a week's worth of clothes over." "Do you think that that might make you more comfortable?" "I'll go home very early on Friday mornings to take care of everything at home, then return to you on Friday evenings after work." Sheila smiled and said, "Thank you, Terrence, we'll try that and see." "I just love you, so, so much". "Terrence, every woman should experience the kind of love and understanding you exhibit in our relationship." Terrence said, "Any woman that is remotely as kind and loving as you will receive well-deserved love and understanding from someone special, too. Then they held each other and began kissing like never before.

Meantime, Angelica had immediately gone to work on her plans for the disappearance of Sheila. She found a real estate firm that specialized in lots of out of the way properties in secluded areas. When the Broker sent Angelica pictures of this one massive property in Nebraska and told her how far from civilization it was, Angelica had a straw purchaser put an all cash offer on the property, to close in ten days. Although the offer was more than one hundred thousand dollars less than the $800,000 asking price, it was accepted and the deal closed in three days. Angelica had already pulled $1,550,000 out of her off-shore account for the purchase and renovations of a property in a very secluded, extremely wooded area, many miles from any small one horse town. The son and daughter of the deceased owner of that property sold the property for so much less than the appraised value because it had already been on the market over three years, since their father's death. His children knew they would never consider living or doing anything there and felt that their dad was the only person that wanted a property in such an isolated place like that. They were happy to get rid of this "White Elephant" that demanded their upkeep in such an out-of-the-way, lost-to-civilization place.

Meanwhile, on Friday evening when Terrence was to bring enough clothes for a week to Sheila's house, around 4:00 PM, Angelica had Sheila sedated and blind folded by two kidnappers that her personal assistant had hired to do her dirty work.

But about 6:00 PM, when Sheila did not answer Terrence's phone calls, he became a bit concerned, but thought she might have just gone to the store or somewhere else to pick up something before he was to arrive at her house at 7:00 PM. Terrence thought, "Perhaps, Sheila got so busy getting her hair done and doing everything preparing for him, maybe time had just slipped away from her." At 7:15, Terrence knew something was definitely wrong, because Sheila would have contacted him by that time, even if she had to use a pay phone or someone's phone in a nearby business.

By 7:45 PM, Terrence could wait no longer. He rushed over to her house and found her front door open and he went in, while calling her name, "Sheila, Sheila, Sheila, darling, where are you?" Her shoes and jacket were on the kitchen floor, but nothing else seemed out of place. Terrence stayed over at Sheila's place from Friday night until Saturday afternoon. By Saturday evening, when the realization hit him that Sheila was really gone, he was so hurt, nervous and upset, he had to be sedated and hospitalized for two days. However after Sheila had been missing 24 hours, her parents filed a missing person's report and offered a $10,000 reward to anyone who knew anything about their daughter's disappearance. But after Terrence's two day hospital stay, he remained at home for two weeks, in case Sheila tried to contact him there. When he did not hear from her, after three weeks, Terrence decided to go back to work, because his working on lawns was the only thing that kept him going.

Meantime, at 11:30 PM on the Friday when Sheila was kidnapped, her abductors had flown her to Nebraska in a rented private plane of an associate of one of Angelica's father's friends. The abductors took Sheila to the secluded house Angelica had purchased and renovated, where she was put to bed. Angelica also paid a forger to duplicate Sheila's signature that Terrence knew so well. The forger wrote letters, in what seemed to be Sheila's handwriting and signed them with what looked exactly like her signature to Terrence with no return address. These letters supposedly explained to Terrence why she left him. The first letter was apologetic and stated that she was so very sorry, but she had fallen in love with another man and had left town to start a new life with him.

Of course this was preposterous to Terrence; completely absurd. He did not/could not believe any of this tripe because he knew that he and Sheila were soul mates who loved each other with all of their hearts. Believing that Sheila had left him for somebody else would be like punching and pulling very large, jagged, ugly holes out of their life-long perfect, loving relationship, leaving it ragged and frayed. This just made no sense to Terrence nor their parents or their friends. However after the first handwritten letter, Terrence started receiving many weekly, apologetic typewritten letters, still with no return address, but signed with Sheila's definitely recognizable signature. After more than a year since Sheila's disappearance and Terrence's daily searching for her and with the letters continual coming now telling him how happy she was with her new love, Terrence began to question: "Could this have really happened. If so, Why? Is this the reason Sheila had begun to act so different, so nervous, so anxious to be with me every waken moment, maybe trying to fight her feelings for someone else. Where and when did I drop the ball? Why and how could a love so strong fail so miserably; for what reason – another man?" "Who is this man? What does he have that I don't?" He certainly could not love her more than I. "None of this makes any sense to me." But the main question is, "How could Sheila have hurt me like this without even a discussion before making a decision to throw everything that we had, away." "Could Sheila really love someone else as much or more than she loved me?" The more Terrence thought about this insanity, the less understanding and/or acceptance of this humongous lie came forth.

Terrence's and Sheila's parents (especially Sheila's) were worried sick over Sheila's disappearance, too. Terrence tried not to cause more stress on their parents than they were already suffering, by not discussing Sheila's disappearance with them every day. Terrence stayed in a state of upset himself, so he had a horribly hard time trying to encourage them so he started only talking with them two or three times a week, instead of everyday, as before.

Terrence found himself presenting all of his hurt and discussing all of his confusion and disconcerted feelings with his understanding and always available friend, Angelica Gamble. Because of all of the needed understanding and comfort Angelica and Terrence willingly gave each other, they became extremely close – as close as Terrence would allow Angelica to get to him. Because of Terrence's loneliness and need for comfort, he would on some few occasions meet Angelica at a restaurant or even a small café after he got off work. She greeted him by first holding his hands, then giving him a hug when they met and a good bye hug before they parted. Although they remained very close friends for a very long time, Terrence still kept a certain amount of distance because that was the kind of person he was with everybody, except Sheila.

One day when Terrence felt extremely low, for some unknown reason, Angelica just happened to be near his neighborhood and she called him and detected sadness in his voice. She said, I am very close to your neighborhood and I can come by, if that is OK with you? He said, Angelica, "I really don't feel like entertaining anybody at this time." She said, "I'll just bring you a bite to eat and I'll only stay until you feel better." "This is what friends do, you know." He finally said, "OK, Angelica and he gave her his address and allowed her to visit him at his home only on that one occasion. She picked up one of his favorite dishes at one of his favorite restaurants in the area that he had told her about. She handed the food to him when he opened the door for her, when she arrived at his home. He thanked her for the meal, but did not eat it right then. Her visit was short as she had promised. She only stayed ten or fifteen minutes until she got a faint smile out of him, then she got a hug from him, before leaving. But Angelica took that one time visit to mean she could call and return whenever she wanted to. So on another day, about two weeks later, Angelica called when she was near his neighborhood again with a scheme she had conjured up, saying she just wanted to come by to pray with him to ask God to return Sheila to him. To this, he said, "Yes, sure you can come, in maybe an hour." But in only about twenty minutes, just after Terrence had finished showering, brushing his teeth, putting on his briefs, a robe and his house shoes, Angelica rang the doorbell several times. Terrence opened the door and said, "Hi, what's the urgency?" "Am I early," Angelica asked, as she walked through the door. "I felt like the sooner we pray for Sheila to come back to you, the better." "Terrence, I heard that if two or more people are joined in prayer, God is in the mist. At this, Terrence said, "That's true, so yes, we certainly can pray, right now. They sat on his sofa, held hands, bowed their heads and she began to pray after clearing her throat, ah hum, ah hum, ah hum then said, "God we know that you can do whatever you want to; so bring Sheila Smith back to Terrence so he won't be so sad. Thank you, God, Amen.

Terrence thinking this was a sincere prayer, said, "Amen", too. When Terrence put his arm around Angelica to hug and thank her, she turned her face to his at the same time and they somehow began to kiss. Terrence pulled back and said, "No, Angelica, this is wrong." But she said, "Yes, this is so right for us; this is what I have been wanting for such a long time." "Terrence, I need you so much." Angelica was so into the sweetest kiss she had ever had, there was no stopping her now. Seems like in an instant, she had taken all of her clothes off, untied the belt on his robe, pushed him back on the sofa and jumped on top of him. He picked her up and carried her to his king size bed and gently laid her down behind him, while he stepped out of his house shoes, took off his robe and his briefs. After seeing all of his beautiful parts, Angelica got so excited, she jumped on him and straddled him saying, "Terrence, I need you so badly," But this strong, masculine, manly man who liked to be on the top and in control of the sex act, gently flipped her on her back, climbed on top of her and held her hands with his against the headboard. Without using his hands nor letting her use hers, he started moving his penis all around the outside of her vagina, pressing gently and sometimes putting it right at her entrance, then moving it and pressing it against her clitoris. He performed this ritual a few times until Angelica thought, "With all that he has, he doesn't even know what to do. I will certainly have a wonderful time teaching him, though." Before she could complete that thought, in that second, Angelica felt like she was on fire, burning with desire for sex like never before. She was so extremely wet and sexually aroused, she started begging, please, please give it to me now, please. "Terrence, please!! I am so ready for you." Then Angelica thought, "What the Hell is this?" "My, my, my, my God this man knows what to do better than anyone else. He has actually set my soul on fire". After he finally pushed his hips forward, penetrating her and they really got into it, he raised his body up; put his hands behind her back lifting her body with his until he was sitting on the heels of his feet, then he placed her legs around him, straddling his hips, causing her to sit up high. He had changed their position while remaining inside of her and never missing any of his slow, deep, forceful, calculating strokes and thrusts. Being up so high in this position, Angelica felt like a cowgirl riding a steer and needed a rodeo hat that she could snatch off, fling in the air and yell, "**Yeaaa Hoooo**". In a few minutes, Terrence flipped himself around onto his side around to the foot of the bed, flipping Angelica on her side at the head of the bed. They were facing the wall, still straddling each other. His right leg was stretched out near her face and she was lying on his left leg that was under her back. Her left leg was under his body and her right leg was behind him. They were holding hands and they never missed a stroke while he remained inside of her. In this position, they resembled two pairs of crisscross scissors. Every time Terrence rolled over, he lifted her body around with his, while remaining inside of her and never missing a stroke, thrust, or gyration. After several more roll overs and flips, Angelica felt that Terrence had turned her every way, but loose. She knew of nothing she had ever read or heard about that could compare to the thrill of the ecstasy she experienced from the acrobatic moves and gyrations performed in this beautiful, intriguing, wonderful love making session with her man, Terrence Watson. All she knew was she was thrilled incessantly as she sometimes purred like a kitten, roared like a lion and screamed like a cage of monkeys in pleasure, as she reached climax, after climax, after climax; perhaps four in all. Angelica thought to herself, Oh my God, I had no idea that I could be multi-orgasmic. But when she tried to say something, her tongue seemed heavy and her words were jumbled, when she said, "Ah cont thro baw tee, ah, la, ha, ha. She actually spoke in an unknown language as though she was speaking in tongue, what some religions call that kind of religious conversing. But Angelica realized that Terrence had just simply thrilled her out of her mind. After a few more rolls, flips, thrusts and gyrations, Terrence moaned and finished. Angelica was as limp as a dish rag, but managed to reach and find Terrence's face to hug and kiss him before falling asleep. However, during their interlude, Terrence called Sheila's name, at least twice. When Angelica woke up, although she remembered that Terrence had called Sheila's name, instead of hers, that was her least concern right then. Angelica could only think of how remarkable sex with Terrence was. Angelica had envisioned so many times how sex with Terrence would be. But in her wildest imagination, she could have never dreamed, foreseen or predicted anything like the thrilling sexual ecstasy she encountered making love with certainly **her man** now**,** Mr. Terrence Watson**.** Angelica was completely immersed in how soon she could begin having this kind of lovemaking for the rest of her life.

Terrence's feelings about their sexual encounter were quite different than Angelica's. He felt like he had been unfaithful to Sheila and had perhaps committed a crime or a sin. When Angelica turned over and saw him sitting on the side of the bed, fully dressed, he turned and looked at her and said, "We made a horrible mistake, Angelica, but this must never happen again, because you are a married woman and I feel like I am cheating on Sheila. Angelica only addressed what Terrence said about her being a married woman. To that statement, Angelica said, "I will start divorce proceedings tomorrow. I will go to Reno and get an overnight divorce. "Terrence, I have never had anything so remarkably good before. I am so in love with you." "Whoa, whoa, wait just a minute," Terrence said. "We love each other as friends only, but we are not in love with each other". "I am not and will never be out of love with Sheila". "Although she has been gone for more than two and a half years, I will never love anyone else the way that I love her and I am still waiting for her to return to me someday. And I will never believe that cock-and-bull story about her leaving me for another man. I truly believe that for some strange, ridiculous reason, someone took my Sheila and probably still has her captive. Therefore, don't you dare divorce Jonathan for a relationship with me, because if I don't marry Sheila, I will probably never live with nor marry anybody else. Besides that, Angelica, "You need to take much more time before considering divorcing a man that you have loved through so many hard times." "Didn't Jonathan explicitly tell you that he has already changed in an effort to save his marriage? Perhaps this time, he means it". "He might mean it this time but it's too late", she said. Terrence said, "Just don't do anything that you'll look back at and have daily guilt feelings and regret over; thinking you did not do all you should or could have done to save your marriage". "OK Terrence, perhaps, you're right, is what she said. But after enjoying such thrilling sexual ecstasy with Terrence, she had not, for one minute given up on the idea of a lifetime relationship with Terrence **(her man).** Angelica was more hell-bent on completely having Terrence now than she'd ever been after engaging in the sweetest, best sex she never could have imagined or ever thought existed.

"Well then", Angelica continues, "I'll try separating from Jonathan for a while without my father knowing about it." Terrence said, "That's going to be hard to do, but I have faith in you because, after almost seven years of marriage, you kept quiet the fact that you were unhappy because of Jonathan's cheating and being unfaithful to you. Then Terrence thought, "You never let out a hint that you had a very close **black** friend as he smiled and wondered to himself, how upset would her father be if he knew **(his baby girl)** had a **black** friend, especially a **black male friend.**" Angelica said, "even so, I still need to divorce Jonathan because I no longer love him, at all". "You and I can continue to see each other and if sex happens, so be it" because you have needs and so do I". And yes, as much as Terrence tried to restrain her, she was determined and sex between them did happen two more times because they spent so much time together. After that third time, Terrence firmly put his foot down and told Angelica that he would stop talking to or spending time with her if she ever put her hands on him again. Although Angelica said, I won't ever make advances to you again. She was definitely not willing to give up this man that she loved more than she could have ever imagined loving someone in her wildest dreams. She never knew feelings like these could exist. Angelica went back to the drawing board. "What could she do to win Terrence over; make him love her enough to have sex with her again and eventually be with her forever?" Angelica offered him money. She said, "I can make you a very rich man." "You can have it all." To this, Terrence said, "no thank you." "I don't even want to be rich." "Being rich seems to cause more problems than I am willing to deal with." She then offered to partner with him in his or some other business or to buy him other businesses and when he said no, she told him he could pay her back on an interest free or very low interest rate loan." His answer to all of her offers was a definite, no. You see, as he had told her, becoming rich was not one of his goals. Living comfortably with the love of his life, Sheila Smith would constitute a life of happiness for him. That was all he dreamed about; all he wanted.

The next day Angelica called Jonathan and told him that she was willing to have a trial separation from him for six month then see how she felt at that point. Jonathan did not like her decision, but what could he do? He said, "Alright, darling, if that is what you want". "We will do it your way". "I am so sorry that I was such a fool". "I hope that you can forgive me this last time". Angelica just ignored what Jonathan was saying and told him, "I will stay away from the house tomorrow and the day after so you can remove all of your belongings including yourself before I return on the third day". Jonathan did as she requested.

Meanwhile for a little more than three years Sheila remained in captivity, but Angelica made sure Sheila was well taken care of in this very quaint, quite lovely, elegantly decorated, large ranch house that sat almost two miles back with one mile of trees on the acreage in front of the house that made it virtually impossible to be seen from the very seldom traveled frontage road. The 15 ft. high fence around the property covered, at least two and a half acres surrounding the house. Sheila was guarded 24 hour a day. She had a cook who prepared her daily meals fit for a king (queen) and a maid that kept the house spotless – doing some cleaning every day. A grounds man who manicured and maintained the grounds and planted the most beautiful flowers inside the fence and kept all the acreage around the house immaculately clean and pretty. There was also a young woman, Marian that Angelica's assistance hired to purchased everything she thought Sheila needed, from personal women's items, even make-up and many, many lovely clothes, including undergarments, dresses, skirts, blouses, panty hoses, shoes and boots, coats and hats, even mink, fox and other fur ones and anything else that Sheila pointed out in fashion magazines that were brought to her with the name on the front of the books always torn off. Marian was also Sheila's personal trainer who walked the grounds daily, inside the fence with Sheila, after their exercise sessions, even on cold or rainy days. All of the people who worked at this house were very well paid and sworn to secrecy.

Sheila had everything she needed including any kind of music she could play on a CD Player. She could not have a TV or a house phone or a radio. Her communications with the outside world were completely cut off. She could only talk with the people hired to guard her and make her comfortable. But Sheila never stopped praying and trusting that God would somehow, someday get her out of this strange, ugly situation. She ordered many, many clothes for herself so she would have everything that she needed, in case her abductors had destroyed all of her things whenever God made sure she was returned to her life with Terrence. Since Sheila felt sure she would someday leave this place, when she was not exercising or walking with Marian, she spent time each day listening to music, mostly gospel, reading, mostly the bible, dancing and singing and praising God, then relaxing in the evening. After a year or more, Marian and Sheila began to talk and share things about themselves. They learned that they both had a very strong belief in God and they became friends that trusted each other and shared more things and when they were sure no one was looking, they prayed together. Marian asked Sheila why she was being kept in this secluded place. Sheila said, "That's a million dollar question. I would love to know that myself." "I thought maybe you or some of the people who work here might know." "Because all I know is I was in my kitchen, preparing dinner for Terrence and I when two men broke into my home, put a bag over my head and I woke up here in bed with a splitting headache that lasted three days. When they first brought me here, I was so afraid, but no one has ever tried to hurt me. "Where is this place?" Nervously, Marian said, "I am not actually sure, but we are all sworn to secrecy and can never tell you that, even if I could find out". "We have been told that something bad will happen to any of us who take care of you if we tell you anything about this place." "But to be honest, none of us really know its exact location". "And none of us know why you are here, either." Sheila said, "Oh Marian, you are my only friend and I would never want anything bad to ever happen to you." "I depend on your friendship, prayers, smiles and kindness to help keep me strong." I will never ask any questions about this place again." Besides that, I know that God loves me and will get me out of this mess when the time is right." So they went back into the house and Marian put all of the exercise equipment away and she and Sheila started back talking and looking again at more clothes and magazine articles. At night fall, Marian went to her room to go to bed, but could not rest. That night, Marian was awake all night, and for weeks she thought about Sheila's predicament and prayed for God's guidance on how to help her friend get out of this horrible situation that no true loving Christian should be in. One month later, as Marian and Sheila were taking their daily stroll around the inside of the fence that surrounded the hidden property Marian said, "Sheila, I feel so sorry for you." "I have been thinking what I could possibly do the help you." "But when I go home each month, I have to spend most of my time visiting my aunt in the nursing home and taking care of all of her needs for the next month as well as checking on and seeing that everything at my home is taken care of. "But I am going to sneak you a pen and a piece of paper." "Write Terrence a note and include his home and business addresses and phone numbers and when I have my three days off at the end of the month, I will try to get him your message. I'll try to call him, but I can't leave him messages because my incoming phone calls are monitored so he can't return my call nor leave me a message. Also, my purse and all of my pockets are checked before I leave and when I return each month but they don't check the underside of my insoles of my shoes." "My God, what happens if you get caught with that note, Marian?" To be honest with you, Sheila,

"I am very frightened, but I know God wants me to help you." The day before Marian was to be escorted to the private plane that carried and returned the employees from their three days off, Sheila sneaked the note to Marian that she had written to Terrence. Marian pulled up one of her insoles and hid Sheila's note in her shoe.

Sheila whispered, "thank you Marian." "I will be praying for you until you return safely." "In fact, I will start praying right now." "Thank you God for sending my friend Marian to me and please protect her as she delivers my message to Terrence." Please go with her and bring her back safely." "Thank you, thank you, thank you, Dear God. Amen, Amen."

For more than three years, Sheila wondered why she had been kidnapped and by whom. She missed Terrence terribly; thought about him every day and dreamed about him almost every night. She prayed for his good health and that he was not kidnapped, too. Sheila longed to hear his warm, loving voice, see and kiss her man so she could feel safe in his arms, again.

While Sheila lived in wonder, as to why she was kept in this place, Angelica became more and more curious about Sheila. She thought daily,

"She is black and a mere, underrated middle class person; I am well educated, pretty, **White and Rich.**" "How does she look?" "Is she prettier than me?" "I know she is couldn't be any smarter than I." "Why couldn't Terrence be in love with me instead of longing for and remaining in love with that long-lost, nappy-headed stupid, black bitch, Sheila Smith?

"Well, I guess I must see for myself?" Angelica made up her face to perfection, put on her $2,000 per ounce perfume that she wore on very special occasions, especially whenever she thought she would see Terrence. She wore one of her finest, most expensive outfits, the most elegant shoes with a matching purse before boarding the private plane she had rented with a pilot with an expert flight record. Then Sheila set out to find out what it was about this Miss Sheila Smith that was so damned captivating to the man who was clearly supposed to belong to her.

The day before Angelica went to see Sheila, Marian had told Sheila that although she was unable to reach Terrence by phone, she had left Sheila's message in his mail box. Hearing this good news, Sheila became so happy that her appearance changed; she became extremely lovelier than ever. Her face was glowing and she wore a smile that could not be erased by anyone or anything. The next day when Angelica arrived at the secluded property and turned her key in the door and walked in and saw this lovely, well dressed black woman glowing, smiling and singing while rocking in the plush, brown mahogany leather chair that sat in the middle of the room. Angelica was immediately enraged with jealousy and anger. Sheila was shocked when Angelica loudly announced to her, **"I am pregnant by Terrence." "He belongs to me now and he will never be yours again."** Although Sheila was astounded and sat there in disbelief, she mustered up enough voice to ask, "Who are you and what are you talking about?" Angelica said, I am Angelica Parker/Gamble, the future wife of Terrence Watson when I tell him that we're going to have a baby. Sheila thought, then said, "Oh, Angelica, the woman that so desperately needed a friend to talk with; **My Terrence**."

At this, Angelica grabbed Sheila by the hair and pulled her up out of the rocking chair and said, "I am going to have you killed, what I should have already done." "Terrence is mine, do you hear me, **MINE!!!** "You'll never see him again; you crazy, stupid, black bitch. Angelica then swiftly turned and ran out of the house and boarded the private plane outside to return home to make plans for Sheila's demise. Angelica did not know that Marian had hidden in the closet, behind the door and saw and heard everything. Marian did not know what to do, but she knew she had to do something to save her friend, Sheila. Marian rushed out of the closet and grabbed Sheila by both hands and the two women began to pray with much reverence and devotion, pleading, believing and trusting that God would answer their heartfelt, sincere prayer this time.

Since Angelica had made a definite decision to have Sheila killed, she had to develop a new strategy, since she was now determined to get rid of the love of Terrence's life for good. No one else could possibly spoil her plans for having Terrence, except this boring, dull, lost-in-time, stupid, black bitch, **Sheila Smith**. Angelica had left out very abruptly, to notify the pilot that she was going back home. As soon as she returned home she put all of her plans for Sheila's murder in motion. She contacted her assistant who was to make all of the arrangements; contact the hit man; make flight arrangements there and back with Sheila's body; order instructions for cremation and how to dispose of Sheila's ashes – all of this was to be done in a certain time frame. A final call from Angelica would start the ball rolling to end all of this; Terrence loving and wanting Sheila Smith only, once and for all.

The only other thing Angelica had to do after returning home was to try to contact Terrence and persuade him to meet with her. Terrence had had so much trouble cutting all communications with Angelica, he no longer answered his phone when he heard her voice. But after Angelica called his number at least ten times right behind each other, he decided to listen to the message, in case there was some kind of a business emergency. After hearing her message that said, "I have good news about Sheila." Terrence immediately returned her call and she asked him to meet her at a restaurant downtown and she would tell him the news about Sheila. Although what Angelica said made Terrence nervous and he was very skeptical as to the truth of her message, but he had to see her to know. When they met at the restaurant that evening, she was so excited, he could tell. "Thinking this might be some of her deceptive tricks, Terrence cautiously asked, "Why are you so anxious today, Angelica"? "Well I have good news for us". "First, I must divorce Jonathan, now". This statement almost threw Terrence off, but he tried to stay focused so he said, "But, you don't want your father to harm him, do you?" I no longer care about that anymore", she said. "But a murder on your conscience, can you live with that", Angelica? She said, "Be quiet Terrence. I have something very important to tell you". Terrence asked, "OK, what is it." "Is it about Sheila?" Angelica said with happiness and excitement, "We are going to have a baby!! I am three months pregnant. I found out a few days ago." Terrence started to stand, but flopped back down in the chair with his eyes bucked and his mouth opened. When he was finally able to speak, he asked, "What did you say?" Angelica said it another way, "Terrence, you and I will, in six months be parents to a beautiful baby that we can love and care for. "Aren't you happy about the good news", she asked?" "This is not good news. It's terrible news, Angelica". "I don't love you and will never love you the way a couple having a baby should". "Like I have always told you, we could never have been anything but platonic friends." "Don't worry, after the baby comes, you will learn to love me because I know you will already love our baby. Won't you love our baby, Terrence?" "I am sure that I will love the baby, but I will never love you in a way for us to spend our lives together." "I thought you understood that." "Besides, the first two times we were intimate and certainly the third time, a little more than three months ago, you assured me that you were on the pill and that you used the sponge, as well." "Was all of this a lie, Angelica?" "Why were you trying to trick me? "Was this your plan from the beginning?" "Well, you were so hell-bent on loving and having sex only with your lousy little, missing pic-a-ninny fiancée, Sheila Smith, I had to do something." "Well, I am truly sorry Angelica, but I have no intentions of making a life with you, now or ever." "OK, but I will see to it that you will never have a life with your beloved Sheila Smith, either." "Terrence, grabbed her arm and said, what do you mean, "You will see to it that I will never have a life with Sheila." "Do you know where she is?" "Angelica, do you know where Sheila is?" "I'll never tell you, Terrence" and she slumped forward in the chair where she sat and began crying with both hands covering her face. Terrence, thought, "Lord, this is all my fault; Sheila is somewhere in trouble because of my having an unnecessary, unwanted relationship with Angelica; because of my stupid unfaithfulness." "I know what I can do." He left the restaurant running as fast as he could. He stopped in front of a business around the corner from the restaurant went in to use their phone. He took out Angelica's father's business cards that she had given him to use as a design for his lawn care service business cards.

Luckily, when Terrence called the main number on the card, a male voice answered and said, "If this is not an emergency or if you are not a personal friend, please hang up and call my business number at ...... "Terrence said in a loud, terrified voice, **"Mr. Parker!! Mr. Parker!! This is an emergency. Please answer the phone!!**

"Your daughter (Your Baby Girl), **Angelica is in serious trouble!!"** "Mr. Parker immediately answered his phone and said, "Who is this"? Terrence, said "Sir, you don't know me, but my name is Terrence Watson." "I am the owner of the lawn care service that manicures the lawn at Angelica and Jonathan Gamble's home in Minnesota." "Your daughter, Angelica Gamble knows the whereabouts of my fiancée, Sheila Smith and is involved in causing Sheila harm."

"I don't know who you are, but I resent and forbid you lying on my daughter like that" "I know that My Baby Girl has never or would not ever harm anyone." "I don't know what you want, but you get off my phone, **Right Now**." "Wait, wait, Mr. Parker, please don't hang up". "Hold on." "Your daughter is pregnant and is not thinking rationally right now." "Right now, she is capable of who knows what?" "I tell you, she is not thinking normally at this time". "Please, just call her right now and ask her where Sheila Smith is?" "Maybe you can keep her from taking part in harming someone, maybe even herself." At this, Mr. Parker said, "This had better not be some kind of hoax or I will find you and you'll be sorry for pulling such a senseless prank. Do you hear me?" Terrence, said, "Yes sir, please just call her this minute and see if Your Baby Girl will tell you where Sheila Smith is so someone can return her safely and keep your daughter from getting into more serious trouble than she can handle." Nothing had ever frightened Leonard Parker like what Terrence had just told him. Mr. Parker's hands were trembling so much, he could hardly dial his phone. What Terrence said shook Mr. Parker from his emotional foundation. He told

Terrence, "I'll call you back at this number in my phone after I talk with my daughter." Angelica was still crying and sniveling when she answered her phone, thinking it was Terrence, she said, "Hel, hel, hello, "I'm glad you called back". But the second her father heard her voice, because he was so terribly afraid, he did not wait to hear what else Angelica was about to say. Using an extremely loud, trembling voice, Leonard Parker talked to (his baby girl) in a way he had never done before, in this loud voice, using words she certainly had never heard directed at her, **"Young lady, just stop all of that stupid, foolish crying, sniffing and sniveling right now." "Do you hear me?" "I mean Right Now!! and I don't want any shit out of you, Angelica. You answer me, immediately and truthfully, right now". "Do you hear me?"** " She said, "Oh daddy, I need to talk to you". "He said, **"I'm going to talk, first. "Are you pregnant? And Who in the hell is Sheila Smith?" and where is she?"** "Daddy, daddy, yes I am carrying your grandchild." "I am a little more than three months pregnant now. Isn't that good news, daddy?" "Yes, that is the best news ever." "Go on, Angelica, **"Who is and where is Sheila Smith?"** After much stammering and stuttering, Angelica finally said, Sheila Smith is in a safe place." "She is a friend of a friend of mine." **Angelica, I want you to send that woman back to Terrence Watson, your lawn care service man, right away. "You do know him and how to get her back to him, don't you?"** Angelica said, "Yes daddy, I know him", with tears running down her cheeks, wondering how she was going to actually get her Terrence back. Angelica feared that after Sheila was returned, she might never get to see and hold Terrence again. But she knew when her father told her to do something, she'd better do it and right away, at that. She thought since she was pregnant with Terrence's baby, maybe she would not lose him completely. Until the child becomes an adult, in 18 to 21 years, she felt she could possibly conjure up a few opportunities to enjoy laying on him and putting her arms around his beautiful body when she had sex with him again. All she knew was she loved him so much, she was willing to wait and see.

Afterwards, with much pain in her heart, Angelica, reluctantly called her assistant to let the assassins and the pilot know to cancel the plans for the murdering of Sheila Smith. The pilot was to now take Sheila back to the private airport in Minnesota and put her in a limo and have the limo driver drop her off in front of the Hilton Hotel in Minnesota and pay $500 to the man in a navy blue and white pinstriped suit, wearing sunglasses standing in front of the Hilton and he will spin her around, then quickly take her blindfold off before running away. After you watch him spend her around and run away, you calmly drive away. Since her vision will be distorted for a few seconds, she won't see who did this. Angelica also called Terrence to tell him the place and time where he could retrieve his fiancée. She warned him, that things would not go according to plan if he arrived even one minute early. Terrence followed her instructions to the letter and found his beloved fiancée, trembling and rubbing her eyes in front of the Hilton, while waiting for him. After Terrence and Sheila saw each other, he consoled, hugged and kissed her. He took her home and they hugged and kissed all night long. Even though they could not make up for lost time, that night they certainly tried as they began to enjoy the most exciting time of their lives.

Sheila and Terrence had lots to talk about the

next morning, especially Terrence's unfaithfulness and about the baby that Angelica was carrying. Terrence told Sheila, "I am so, so, so very sorry for the mess that I got you into because of my foolish unfaithfulness." "I know that I am the reason that you were kidnapped and held captive for so long". "And although I know that you deserve better than what I did to you, I hope and pray that you can find it in your heart to forgive me." "Sheila please give me another chance." "There is no one else that I have ever or will ever love, want or need the way I do you." "I sure hope that you know this." Sheila's mature answer was, "I have and will always love you with all of my heart, Terrence." "I know you have been and always will be faithful to our relationship, but I was gone for three years without you knowing when or if I would ever come back to you. Plus, you had no experience with anyone so spoiled and determined to make you **hers** at any cost." "Terrence, I have already forgiven you." "We belong together."

After much embracing, kissing and love making, the next afternoon, Terrence and Sheila applied for their marriage license and two days later went to the Justice of Peace and got married on Valentine's Day, February 14, 1998, instead of February 14, 1994, as they had originally planned. The next day when further discussing their plans for their future, Sheila said, "We have to decide what to do about our baby that Angelica is carrying." "Well", Terrence said, "I don't know if or how we can even ever see the child, since it's imperative that we stay away from Angelica, forever". "At this time, all we can do is pray for the baby and for Angelica's mental health so she can properly care for the child", Terrence finally said.

"Sheila, my love, you know that we must move out of this area of the country as soon as possible, don't you?" Sheila said, "What will we do about your business?" "Oh, selling the lawn care business won't be hard to do." "I just hate to have to let go of my devoted employees." "In the next two weeks before we leave, I'll try to set them up with other companies". "Sheila, don't you worry, because for some reason, somebody has deposited lots of extra money into my account and we now have more than enough money to live off of for three, four or maybe even five years without working as well as enough to buy the best equipment to start our new business with a new name wherever we decide to live." "Isn't it wonderful that we can take our time to find the right location for our new home and business?" Sheila said, "Yes darling, I am truly happy, but we can't help wondering, where all of that extra money came from? Are you sure it is ours and we can keep it without getting arrested, sometime in the future? Maybe someone put it in your account by mistake; do you think?" The bank branch manager checked the records and assured me that all of it is mine, free and clear. "OK, since you checked and are sure, that's wonderful, Terrence." "Oh my, I had forgotten to check at my bank to see if my savings and investments are still there or if someone has taken them." They immediately went to the bank to withdraw her approximately $50,000 CD investments and small savings. But when they got to her bank, they found that two months before, some undisclosed benefactor had made exorbitant deposits, with her name on them, into her account, totaling a little more than $950,000. They were so extremely shocked, they took no chances, they checked with the bank president and he assured them that the amount was correct and all hers, but that the benefactor left explicit instruction that the beneficiary could never be told who left this gift. All of this money put them in such a much better financial position than they could have never, ever imagined. Even though they were very curious, as to where the money came from, they were also extremely excited and happy. They got back in his car, held hands and prayed to thank God for choosing them for such an enormously huge miracle and blessing. Since they could now truly live anywhere in the United States or most any other country, this made it even harder for them to decide where they would live. But after much prayer and discussion, they finally chose Pasadena, California where with his outstanding landscaping experience, Terrence would have plenty of work creating beautiful lawns there, as he did in Minnesota. Although Terrence and Sheila had no idea of Logan's existence, ironically Pasadena, California was only a 5 hrs. 45 minute drive to San Francisco where Logan had lived with his adopted parents, James and Jacqueline Jones, since they adopted him from the orphanage at four months old.

Six months after Angelica and Jonathan's separation, she allowed him to return home. By then Jonathan loved Angelica almost as much as Angelica loved Terrence Watson. Jonathan had proved that he was now completely faithful to his wife. And because he love Angelica so much, Jonathan already loved the baby she was carrying and did not care that he was not the biological father. In the six month, near delivery time, Angelica and Jonathan had become very close, partly because only the two of them knew that he was not their baby's biological father.

Meanwhile, Mrs. Catherine Parker had already been gone three days of a five-day cruise with a women's group that she was a member of, when Angelica started having false labor pains. Leonard Parker answered Jonathan's call, but since Angelica's doctor thought she would not give birth until at least another week Leonard Parker elected not to tell his wife and spoil the last two days of her cruise. But Mr. Parker immediately took a flight to Minnesota and when arrived at the hospital, he saw Angelica's husband, Jonathan coming down the hall with a cup of coffee in his hand. They were happy to see each other so they shook hands and greeted each other and walked to the waiting room together because they had decided to remain at the hospital until the baby was born. It was quite a scene to see Angelica's father sitting with her husband in the waiting room on pins and needles together. After a long while that day, the doctor came to the waiting room with two surprise announcements, telling them, "Mrs. Gamble will deliver her twin sons sooner that we thought. They shouted in unison, "TWINS." Wow, did this make them want to dance and jump for joy. They were still talking and rejoicing over the twins, when the doctor came back in two and a half hours and said, "Mrs. Gamble has had a very hard time and we had to perform a cesarean but she and the babies are doing fine." "Whichever one wants to go in first to visit with Mrs. Gamble and the twins first, come with me." "Just remember she has been through a lot, so only one can visit at a time for only five minutes, please." Mr. Parker said to Jonathan, "No disrespect to you, but that is My Baby Girl and I can't wait any longer, I must go in first." Jonathan did not like this, but what could he do, but say, "I understand."

When Leonard Parker went in the room and smiled at his daughter and said, "You did it." "How are you?" Angelica was so drowsy, she opened one eye and turned her head and went back to sleep. The doctor told Mr. Parker that Mrs. Gamble was basically still unconscious and would probably remain like that the rest of the day and maybe the next day, too.

When Mr. Parker turned and looked at his grandsons, he was so shocked, they were identical, with the same little faces, but one was bald, pale and definitely white. But the other one had a full head of beautiful curly/straight black hair and he was somewhat olive complexion. Instantly, everything became crystal clear to Leonard Parker. He then knew who Terrence Watson was to his daughter, Angelica, and why she was involved in kidnapping and trying to harm Sheila Smith. Leonard Parker requested that the doctor have the nurse retain Jonathan Gamble in the waiting room until he could correct this mistake. But the doctor informed Mr. Parker that his daughter had been informed eight weeks earlier that she would give birth to healthy twin boys. And at that time Angelica told everybody in his office that her first born would be Logan and his brother would be Lucas. Mr. Parker said, "OK, OK, the babies records will reflect that Lucas was born perfectly healthy, but little Logan stopped breathing in the birth canal and could not be revived when he was born. "Since Angelica was unconscious during the delivery, she won't know.

Leonard Parker had never exhibited acts of prejudice against anyone; people he employed, business partners, acquaintances, poor people, people he saw on the streets nor people of any other races. But until the day the twins were born, he had never had an occasion to think about how he would feel about having a black relative.

Leonard Parker's reaction to get his little olive complexed grandbaby out of the picture was without rational thought. He paid handsomely to have the appropriate papers drawn up, authenticating baby Logan's death and burial. Then Mr. Parker had his beautiful little grandson transferred to another extremely expensive, private Hospital in San Francisco, California for four months. He felt baby Logan would be old enough in four months to be adopted. The rules for the baby's adoption were very strict and rigid. Nevertheless every couple and single person, too desired to become this beautiful little baby's parents/parent. The lucky couple selected were the Joneses - James, a Professor at a College nearby their home and his wife Jacqueline, an Executive Assistant at a Proctor and Gambles plant in San Francisco only thirty minutes away from their home.

Meantime, Angelica did not believe it when she was told one of her babies had died. "Not mine and Terrence's baby", she thought. She cried and cried and cried until she could cry no more. For four and a half months, she only ate small **portions of food that was fed to her by her nurse. She mostly slept and stared in space** when she was awake, even when the nurse was bathing, dressing her or combing her hair.

Angelica only brushed her own teeth or used the commode by herself. She never believed that her other baby was dead. She also felt that if Terrence knew about his sons, only he could give her comfort or convince her that one of their babies had died. She thought about Terrence every day and dreamed about him most nights.

She felt it was unfair to have his babies and he never had the opportunity to see or hold them. Angelica just knew in her heart that if he had seen or touched them that would have made a big difference. She wasn't sure what difference; maybe the other one would not have died, if in fact, the baby was really dead. She wondered if the missing baby looked at all like Terrence, she sat silently and yearned for Terrence and their other baby so much, she went into a very deep, dark depression.

No one could; not the best medicine, nor the best psychiatrist in the US, like the one that her father hired, could help bring her out of the situation she now lived in.

Often, when baby Lucas was brought into the room with Angelica, she did not acknowledge his presence. Some other times she would look at him as if she did not know he was hers. And other times, she might look at him and say hello little baby, do you miss your brother?" "I do." Almost every day Angelica looked out of the window to say, "My son is out there, somewhere. Maybe she thought the other baby might be more like his father, Terrence.

In a few months, because baby Lucas' growing in hair was reddish/brown like Angelica's and Mrs. Parker's, everybody raved over how much the baby looked like his mother and/or his grandmother. Listening to what people said about her baby, she began to look at him and she was astonished at what she saw. Although baby Lucas had reddish/brown hair, the way his hair shaped his face, she could see that her baby looked like his father, Terrence Watson. Angelica picked him up, something she had never done before, and began to hug and kiss him. While she was standing, she sang to him as she turned and danced around the floor. The nurse did not want any harm to come to the baby, so she stood up when she saw Angelica reach for him. But happiness filled the nurse's heart when she saw the love and compassion for the baby in Angelica's face. Later, when the nurse reached for the baby to take him back to his room, Angelica said, "Just let him sleep in here in his crib for a while longer." The little one stayed in his crib in the room with his mother just watching him until after 4:00 am.

In the next few days, Angelica began getting up early, bathing herself and eating her breakfast to get ready for the baby to be brought to her. She fed him and changed his diapers and burped him, as well. In a few more days, she started picking out at least two or three cute little outfits for him to wear each day. She began talking and singing to him and hugging and kissing him more and more. But she never forgot to ask baby Lucas if he missed his brother. Most everyone thought Angelica had a mental problem, even if it was a just a slight mental problem, requiring only a mild pill to keep her calm.

Three months after Leonard Parker had left little Logan, he became very conflicted by what he had done to his own, precious little grandchild. Therefore, he hired a private investigator so he could keep up with his grandson's whereabouts. He knew when little Logan was adopted, by whom and where they lived. He had pictures taken of him at varying times and occasions as he was growing up on baby Logan (his grandchild's) birthdays and other special occasions. Whenever he was in other countries, Leonard Parker would send toys and other gifts and large monetary endowments to little Logan with no return addresses. The Joneses, baby Logan's adopted parents wondered who and why in the world this person or these people were sending such large sums of money to their son. They became suspicious that this person or people might someday show up and try to claim him or kidnap their child. Little Logan was already very loved, well-kept and watched daily, but these gifts made the Joneses keep even a more watchful eye over their precious son.

Leonard Parker also had an investigator to keep up with his grandson's biological father, Terrence Watson. He knew when Terrence and Sheila married and where they moved, in case he wanted to send more monetary gifts to them for the injustices they endured by his extremely spoiled daughter, Angelica Lorraine Parker Gamble.

By the time the twins were turning 17 years old, Leonard Parker could not take it any longer. He had lived daily with the horrible thing he had done to his own flesh and blood. Leonard Parker had first began to feel conflicted about what he had done to baby Logan only three months after he had falsified the death of his grandbaby. Mr. Parker often questioned his true motives and wondered why he had done such a horrible thing to his handsome, little innocent grandson. But after 17 years of dealing with all of the guilt and shame, he confessed to his wife, Catherine that they did have two grandson (identical twins). He told her he had falsified the other baby's birth records and vehemently lied about his death and put him up for adoption. "Yes, honey, we do have two grandsons; Logan did not die". "Why in the world did you give our beautiful, little grandson away", she asked. He told her, "Our grandchild is black". To this, she said, "So what". "I'll love him no matter what; why wouldn't you, Leonard?" Leonard Parker immediately realized that if his grandbaby had been born unsightly or with a physical or mental handicap/deformity or any other kind of abnormality, he would love him. So why couldn't he love his own flesh and blood, no matter what. In fact, realization hit him; he already loved little Logan. Why else had he been keeping up with what was going on in that child's life all of these years. All of a sudden, Leonard Parker knew he sent the many gifts and money in an effort to assure that Logan could get the best schooling possible and always have everything that he needed and a bank account that would assure security for him forever. After acknowledging he actually did love his grandchild, he knew he had many, very hard amends to make. He had to tell Angelica that he took her baby from her; beg forgiveness and hope that he would not lose his baby girl, permanently. He had to tell Lucas that the brother his mother often mentioned to him, did actually exist. He had to contact the biological father and let him know that the child he knew existed was actually a twin. But the hardest thing would be explaining to his own grandson Logan, why he discarded him, and yet kept Lucas, his twin brother.

Meantime, now that Mrs. Catherine Parker knew how long her husband had lived in agony with all of this guilt and shame, she insisted that she and Leonard Parker had to go to visit Logan (the name that his adopted parents chose to keep). When Catherine and Leonard Parker contacted Logan's parents, the Joneses were instantly in agreement for a meeting with the Parkers and/or whomever else were part of Logan's beginning. Although the Joneses did not know how the Parker's knew how to contact them, they could not have been more anxious for an audience with these strangers who might have some of the answers to questions that had, somewhat plagued them for seventeen years. They wanted to know who Logan's birth parents were; how they could have given such a beautiful, lovable, happy little baby up for adoption; were they so young or so heartless that they could not have loved and cared for their child; were they alcoholics or drug addicts; were they running away from something or someone. Since their son, Logan had brought nothing but joy into their lives, and the Joneses would never have considered letting their son go with anyone else, but they had all of these unanswered questions from the beginning when they first saw their very handsome little baby at that adoption agency. The Joneses realized that all of their curiosity about these strangers might not be cleared up in a day so they asked the Parker's if everyone would make plans to remain in San Francisco for at least five days. The Parker's said, "Certainly, that is a great idea. We will be happy to stay as long as you have time to let us come to your home to visit with you, Mr. and Mrs. Jones and Logan."

After Mr. and Mrs. Parker learned that the Joneses wanted to get to know anyone from Logan's beginning, Leonard Parker did what he knew was another right thing to do. He also contacted the Watson's, Sheila and Terrence. They too, wanted to meet their son, or as the Parkers' told them---sons (twins). Mr. Parker suggested that everyone bring enough casual clothes for a five day stay in a nearby hotel. Angelica, Jonathan, Lucas Gamble and Leonard and Catherine Parker were all very excited at the thought of meeting and spending time with their son and grandson for the first time. The flight from Houston, Texas to San Francisco was a little over 4 hr. and the Watson's drive from Pasadena to San Francisco was 5 hrs. 45 minutes. Terrence, in his excitement must have driven much faster than he normally did because he and his wife, Sheila, the Gamble's and the Parker's arrived on the Joneses front porch at the same time, as though they had planned the exact minute they were to meet. With no introductions, they only greeted each other with, "Hi" and starring, shocked looks. Then everybody anxiously reached for the door knob at the same time. Mr. and Mrs. Jones heard them and opened the door. They said hello Mr. and Mrs. Jones, we are Logan's other family. The Joneses said, "Oh, really!! Oh, yes, please come in. In the Joneses living room, all of the proper introductions began, then they all began to stare at Logan in shock. The Watson's had already been spellbound on the Joneses porch looking at Lucas who looked a lot like Terrence. Upon entering the house, when Angelica first saw her son, Logan, she ran and grabbed him in a bear hug with tears streaming down her face, all over his shirt. She told him, as she rubbed his handsome face, "Logan, I am your biological mother; I always knew in my heart that you were alive. I love you now; I always have and I always will." "You are so handsome; you look just like I had always imagined you would". Then she reminded him many, many more times, "I love you so much Logan and I want so much to get to spend time with you; and to get to know my first born son". Terrence and Sheila were standing and looking back and forth at everyone, especially the twins. After about three minutes of holding this weeping woman, Logan had to gently but firmly pull away from her because he saw this tall, young man standing perfectly still in the middle of the floor, next to his parents, Mr. and Mrs. Jones. Logan stepped forward, first and the two slowly walked towards each other with their mouths open, in disbelief. Lucas and Logan felt as if they were looking in a mirror as they starred at each other. They had the same face and were the same height, size and build. The only difference was Logan's olive complexion and their hair; Logan's thick curly/straight black hair and Lucas's hair, also thick, but was reddish/brown and straight. They extended their hands in an effort to shake, but jerked each other into a very emotional embrace with tears dripping off their chins. When they pushed back to actually search their eyes and into their souls for a few minutes, they were finally able to speak. As they talked, everyone had to look to see which one was talking because they had the same voice; they sounded exactly alike. They even tried to ask the same questions or say the same things at the same time during their conversations. Everyone in the room, especially the twins were amazed at what they witnessed and they all smiled and laughed out loud with joy watching the brothers interact with each other.

Sheila immediately realized that the twins looked a lot like their father, Terrence and had his same demeanor and mannerisms. The twins recognized the resemblance, too and they just automatically walked over to their biological father for a big family hug and said together, "Hello, Dad." Terrence said, "Hello sons this is your stepmother, Sheila," and they walked over to her and also greeted her with a very warm and amorous hug, while saying, "Hi, mom." Sheila told them, "Hello our handsome sons; our family has just increased because you have a 15 year old brother, Terrence, Jr. and a 13 year old sister, Candice and you'll get to meet them in a couple of months, when both of you have finished school and they are out of school for the summer." "At that time, you can all spend a month or two together at our house, getting to know each other and allowing your father and me to get to know you, as well, if that is OK with your parents. The Joneses and the Gamble's agreed that they needed to get to know each other.

Angelica was so happy to see her two sons and their father together. But this caused a problem within her. Seeing this, her love for Terrence, the father of her very handsome sons, resurfaced with renewed strength. Back to the drawing board, she thought, "How can I possibly get Terrence to spend some quality time with me again because watching Terrence and Sheila's reactions to each other, it was obvious that they were still so happy and so much in love." But they had decided to leave their son and daughter at home and planned to tell them about their two estranged brothers after they decided, how and when they could allow them to meet their siblings and other family members. They knew meeting everyone, especially the twins would be just as or more exhilarating for their children than it was for them. But at the same time, meeting them would present many hard to explain questions for Terrence and Sheila to answer.

Late that evening, after becoming acquainted with everybody, the Joneses felt more relaxed and more comfortable with Logan's extended family so they suggested that it would be much more convenient if everyone spent all five days at their home, instead of in a hotel downtown. Everyone accepted and agreed that at the Joneses house, none of them would have to be separated from each other, at all. The Joneses five bedroom, four and a half bath house could accommodate all of them. They could meet in the kitchen, living room or any other room or rooms in that house, anytime, day or night. They could laugh and talk as loud and/or as much as they wanted without disturbing others. Leonard Parker, especially thought this was an excellent idea, because he had something of utmost importance to share with and confess to them, his family.

Everybody was so happy and excited, they stayed up most of the night, only sleeping two or three hours, then they decided what to order for breakfast. Before the food arrived, they took quick showers, so they could congregate together again in some room after they finished breakfast and straightened up the kitchen. Then, they all went into the living room just laughing and chattering away because they felt compelled to get to know each other as quickly as humanly possible.

While sitting back, just watching his family interact with each other, Mr. Parker became overwhelmed with emotion. All of a sudden, he stood up with his eyes filled with tears and said, "Will everybody be quiet for a few minutes, please?" "I need to confess some things so each of you might better understand who you really are.

Since Catherine Parker was sitting next to her husband, she stood up with him and put her hand on his back and began rubbing and patting him in an effort to console him as his voice cracked and changed and his eyes welded up with more tears. He struggled, but he continued, saying, "I always considered myself to be an honest and trustworthy man. But on the contrary, I was just simply lying to myself, as he sniffed and blew his nose on a napkin that his wife had given him. I owe every one of you an apology for a stupid, impromptu action that I took without thinking rationally, about seventeen years ago that has affected all of your lives." I hope that you can somehow forgive me, but even if you can't right now, I hope that someday you can." He continued, "Umm, umm, umph this is much harder than I thought it would be." "Let's see, Logan when you and Lucas were born, I realized you were black and I panicked simply because I had never thought about having a black relative." As more tears fell, Leonard Parker said, "So Logan, I had records drawn up authenticating your death and burial," as he cried uncontrollably, causing everyone else to cry, as well. But Mr. Parker continued, "Then I foolishly had you sent to another hospital for four months when I felt you would be old enough then to be sent to an orphanage to be adopted by some loving family that looked more like you". By this time, tears were freely flowing down Mr. Parker's face and dropping off his chin. After he had somewhat regained his composure, but still crying and using all the napkins his wife could get her hands on, he said, Logan, my very handsome grandson, I hope you can somehow, someday forgive me now that you know that my actions were not because I didn't love you. Although I didn't know at that time that I loved you, I did and I always have." "I did what I did without thinking, but I have thought a lot about what I did almost every day, since." With tears running down his face, Logan walked over to his grandfather; put his arms around him and said, "Grandfather Leonard Parker, believe me, it's OK", as he hugged Mr. Parker and wiped the tears from his grandfather's eyes; then from his own. "My life with my loving parents has been a very happy and wonderful one." "I couldn't have asked for a better, more rewarding, nor more interesting life. "As far back as I can remember, my parents have told me that I was adopted and we don't know why people make the decisions that they do but God had worked it out for us." "And my parents also taught me that I must forgive because forgiveness is a part of life." "Therefore, forgiving you is a done deal. You are totally forgiven by me, Granddaddy Leonard Parker." "Things can only go up from here; Right?" "Even though I did not know you, Granddaddy Leonard Parker; I knew you existed. I have always loved my birth parents and grandparents because I knew you were out there somewhere." "I often prayed that all of you were still alive and healthy." "And also thank you for allowing Lucas, my identical twin brother and I to finally meet. I already love him and I will pray for him too, every day**." Because of your generosity and many financial contributions to me, through the years, my family and I have had experiences that we would not have been privy to without you." "My parents and I can never thank you enough for all that you have done for us." "Wow, said Mr. Parker, as he began to cry again, "Oh, thank you, thank you, my precious grandson." "Well, well, well," he said, as he took a deep breath, "I didn't expect that", as he patted his eyes with the last remaining napkins on the table and blew his nose for the twentieth time. "I feel like the luckiest person alive, right now." Then, Logan beckoned for Lucas to join him and their grandfather for a long, loving family hug.

Afterwards, when Mr. Parker nervously raised his arm in Angelica, his daughter's direction as he looked at her and said, "My only baby girl, whom I love more than life itself, "umph, umph, umph, ump, It is hard to believe that I could have hurt you like I did; thinking that I had the right to take your baby from you." "You see, Angelica, since you were unconscious when the babies were born, I felt that you would be so proud that you still had one to smother in love, you would adjust to baby Logan's death and just put all of your love and concentration on baby Lucas. I knew you would be hurt by the loss of one of them, but I thought you would cherish baby Lucas so much, you would soon be OK. I had no idea that you would never get over baby Logan's death." Seeing how much you were suffering, I wanted so desperately to undo what I had done, but it was too late." "The Joneses had already adopted our little Logan so I hired an investigator to keep tract of our baby and send pictures showing how well he was doing." Then Leonard Parker broke down again; he was crying so hard, his shoulders bouncing up and down when he said, "I know that you may never forgive me, but I am hoping-against-hope that you will at least, someday be able to look at me without disdain and disgust." Angelica was crying uncontrollably, too when she walked over to her father and said, "Yes, daddy you hurt me with that horrible mistake because you did not think it through. But daddy, "Life has taught me that hurt is out there for everyone, even me; often by people that you are closest to you." "Daddy, you are and have always been the best, kindest, most loving father anyone could ask for. "You have taught me so much; you've given me a wealth of knowledge." "Daddy, I love and respect you so much, I can't let one mistake, no matter how gigantic, keep me from the love and support that you have always given me." "Certainly, I forgive you; you're still my rock. And daddy, "I thank you for giving me the opportunity to get to know Logan, my first born. "Just look at Logan; I can't stop looking at him; he is so handsome just like Lucas." "Daddy, I have never been happier than I am right now." Angelica then hugged and kissed her father and then her mother, as all three of them just stood there crying in a loving embrace. Later, everyone started to wipe tears off their faces and chins.

Mr. Parker, still sniffing and wiping his eyes, turned facing the Watson's, Terrence and Sheila and said, "First Terrence I want to thank you for that call you made to me so many years ago, insisting that I contact Angelica." "I know something terrible might have happened without you persistence." "You're welcome, Mr. Parker," said Terrence. "And likewise, I thank you for calling us about this family meeting and for alerting us to the fact that our son is actually twins (two sons)." "Contacting you about our twins is what I should have done --- much sooner, Terrence." Terrence said, "Also Mr. Parker, the money that you so generously contributed to us has made our lives so much richer." "Thank you so very much." "Oh, that was the least that I could do, after the agony that Angelica, my daughter put you and your poor wife, Sheila through." Sheila chimed in and said, "Mr. Parker we really appreciate all of that money that you gave us, but you shouldn't take responsibility for what your daughter did." "Yes, I know, said Mr. Parker, but I am primarily the one who spoiled her and allowed her to think that she could have whatever she wanted; whenever she wanted it; no matter what the costs." "You see, to that end, I am guilty." Sheila said, "Terrence and I don't see it that way, but we are absolutely happy for your gracious financial gifts and happy that we don't have to give the money back." At this, Mr. Parker laughed and said, "No you don't have to give it back; "I made me feel better to donate something to you for the distress and torment my daughter caused." "I just hope that you are able to forgive me and Angelica for all of the worry and frustration you endured for three whole years." Terrence said, "Well, Mr. Parker, Sheila and I were thinking that since Logan and Lucas are our sons, too and we want them in our lives, non-forgiveness is not an option." "So, yes, Mr. Parker, we definitely forgive you." Terrence and Mr. Parker reached to shake hand, but Sheila stretched out her arms and wrapped them around both men in a big hug and they all smiled and the three of them stood there in that embrace a few minutes. After the hug, Mr. Parker looked around and called out, "Lucas." "Well, there you are, Lucas I had no right to take your brother from you." Lucas quickly interrupted him and said, "Granddaddy, I forgive you for whatever you did to this handsome young man that you gave everything in the world to." "I will continue to love you the way that I always have, if that is OK with you?" "Oh and granddaddy, thank you for giving my twin brother back to me." "Boy, do I like him; and although it's strange, but at the same time it is very exciting to actually meet yourself; It's a surprise worth waiting for." "And thank you for putting this whole family together, at last. "We fit so well; don't you think?" "And I understand that I even have another brother and sister that I am completely anxious to meet, now. Granddaddy, when you do something, it's like nothing else that anyone else can do." "You do it with such emotion, including everybody crying but afterwards, making everybody happier than we have ever been." Then Lucas reached his hand out for Logan to join in the grandfather, grandsons, loving hug. After Lucas finished his speech, everyone was laughing and crying and wiping their faces all at the same time.

But when Mr. Parker looked in Joneses direction, James and Jacqueline threw their hands up and Mr. Jones said, "Don't look at us because we have nothing to forgive anyone for." "We only have love and appreciation in our hearts for all that we have received from this family; the greatest, most handsome son in the world who has been given enough money to last him a life time and these other new, wonderful family members, too." All we can do is extend our gratitude and say, "Thank you, thank you, thank you to all of you." Everyone met in the center of the living room floor for the most heartfelt family hug, ever. Then everybody started back laughing, talking and eating for the remaining of their three days together. When it was time to leave, everyone got their bags, hugged and kissed each other good bye, got into their respective rides and left, waving and throwing kisses, as they drove out of sight.

Although they were very happy on the 5 hr. 45 minute drive home; the Watson's were also filled with mixed emotions as they discussed what they had seen and what and how to tell their children. When they arrived back home, Terrence Jr. and Candice were waiting at the door and started questioning them before they could put their luggage down. Their mother said, "Calm down, calm down, you two. Please, give us a little time; let us catch our breaths for just a few minutes." "We'll meet you in the den in ten minutes. OK?"

After discussing how to begin the conversation, Terrence and Sheila joined their children in the den and said, "Both of you, just please be quiet until we finish. Their mother said, "There is no way to tell you this except to say, you have older twin brothers; one (Logan) is black and the other one (Lucas) is white". Terrence said, "I am their biological father. A little more than seventeen years ago, I made the biggest mistake of my life by being unfaithful to your mother. Because of me, your mother was kidnapped and almost killed by someone and the twins mother probably had something to do with it". "But that was then and this is now." But we just learned last week, there were two babies (twins) instead of one". "Your mother forgave me and holds no grudges, as I hope you can, also." "That is the story in a nutshell." "Do you have anything to say? Any questions?" Terrence Jr. shook his head, "No." Candice said, "Daddy, are our brothers' mother white"? Sheila said, "Yes, she is. But that was a long time ago, so don't judge." "You'll learn more and understand better, in time". They said, in agreement, "We love you daddy and we can forgive you of anything. If you need our forgiveness, you've got it." "Oh, **Mama,** we are so thankful that you were not harmed", while they reached and began hugging and kissing their loving parents." "Thank both of you for getting past that mistake and for having us and becoming our parents. We know that no one in the world has better parents than we do". Then they wanted to know when they could meet their older brothers. Terrence Jr. said, "I just don't know how I will feel about our brothers' mother. Their mother said, "That might be a problem for all of us, son." Angelica was still contemplating how and when she would/could get to see Terrence alone. After more than nineteen years, she had not perished the thought of having him for her very own.

Jonathan, Angelica's husband had loved her through everything, all of these years. He had for many years known that she never loved him again the way she had in the beginning after his many, many extra marital affairs. When he learned that there were really two babies' and saw that the other one was black. And seeing Terrence and the twins at the Joneses house and because of Terrence's striking resemblance to the twins, Jonathan knew Terrence was the twins' biological father. He feared that Angelica might leave him for that tall, handsome, black man who was actually their son's father.

Jonathan had no idea how strong the love between Terrence and Sheila was and had always been. He did not know how Angelica's pregnancy happened. If he only knew that Terrence would have never been intimate with his wife if she had not tricked Terrence into a friendship with her and had caused Terrence's fiancée, Sheila Smith to go missing for more than three years; nor did he know the number and types of tricks Angelica played to get Terrence into bed after more than two and a half years by using her calculated persuasion. If he only knew these things, he would have known that he had nothing to worry about because Angelica nor anyone else had any chance of coming between Terrence and Sheila, who were bound together by unmatched love. Besides that, Angelica knew that her parents would take drastic measures if she ever did anything to any of the Watson's, ever again.

With the Joneses permission, Terrence and Sheila conversed on the phones with Logan at least four to six times a week and Logan and Lucas talked with each other every day, many times, more than once a day. All of them, also sent letters and notes and messages to each other. By three and a half months, the twins and the Watson's had developed a very close relationship.

The time came and the twins went to visit their other family; their younger brother, Terrence Jr. who looked a lot like them and their baby sister, Candice, a true beauty and sweetie pie, as well. They had never enjoyed any summer vacation as much as they did, this one. The love they had for each other was just automatically already in place and they had so much fun and learned all sorts of things about each other. They hated for their time together to end, but it did, seemingly too fast. But not without them making plans to be together again for the Thanksgiving and Christmas holidays. They would enjoy Thanksgiving at the twins mother's and stepfather's house and the twins' grandparents homes at Christmas.

During the five day (Wednesday through Sunday evening) Thanksgiving visit with at the Gamble's, they were so well received and the love from Angelica and Jonathan was almost overwhelming. Because Angelica still loved Terrence so much, and could see his resemblance in all the children to him, it was easy for her to love his children like they were her very own. She and Jonathan treated them like royalty (like Kings and a Queen). The Gamble's enjoyed them so much and did not want them to leave on

Sunday evening. Terrence, Jr. and Candice were returning home but Lucas and Logan were leaving to find a four bedroom apartment to share near the University of California where they would be attending school in January. They needed four bedrooms so if Terrence, Jr. and Candice visited at the same time and wanted to stay overnight, there would be adequate space for everyone to be comfortable and feel right at home. But as Angelica and Jonathan hugged and kissed the kids goodbye, she told them, "Jonathan and I will be waiting, with anticipation for your return". She asked Logan and Lucas, "After you have settled into your new place, and/or need a break from your studies, will it be OK for me and Jonathan to visit or to take you out on the town or to dinner?" They both said, "Yes, that would be nice. We'd like that very much" and they got in the car and left, waving and throwing kisses while Lucas drove them out of sight.

At Christmas, when this foursome (the twins, Terrence, Jr. and Candice) visited the twins' grandparents, they received a very similar reception with kind and loving treatment from Leonard and Catherine Parker. The Parker's loved and accepted Terrence, Jr. and Candice as their biological grandchildren, as well, since both of them always wanted large families with lots of grandchildren and someday many great grands, too. Although the Parker's never included Jonathan Gamble in their wealth, they taught Logan their legal grandson and Terrence Jr. and Candice the Oil business and included them in all of the Parker's wealth. Lucas already knew most of the business and had been included in the Parker's wealth since childhood.

Christmas was the same as Thanksgiving because the seven days (Monday to Sunday evening) had ended much too soon. After the hugs and kisses were over, before the kids got into their rental car, Leonard Parker said, "Let's do this again. Let's meet again next month somewhere (your choice), and this time, maybe you would like to invite all of the parents and spouses, and certainly including James and Jacqueline Jones – Logan's adopted parents. "As a matter of fact, is it OK with everybody if we make our meetings, a monthly vacation (Our Family Thing to Do)? "What-a-you think"? "That's a great idea", they all said in unison, like they were singing a song. "Thanks, granddaddy; grandaddy Leonard Parker; Mr. Parker!!! They got into the car, fastened their seat belts, and looked back, waving, throwing kisses to each other until Logan finally drove away and out of site.

The children could not decide where they wanted to meet the next time. Since it was a very cold winter, Mr. Parker asked them if they would like to meet in Hawaii. The kids responded positively, very quickly, but this idea pleased everyone. This trip could only be for five days, because all of the children were in school. They had to have excuses from school for three days, then include Saturday and Sunday to have enough time to enjoy Hawaii. This very enjoyable trip was well planned by Mr. and Mrs. Parker. Love, contentment and happiness were in the hearts of everyone. They went on excursions, tours, sightseeing ventures and all were given their purchased hula skirts for their chance to hula until their hearts' content.

Surprisingly, during this vacation, almost everybody noticed that Angelica seemed different, somehow. They did not know what the change was, but Angelica paid more attention to her husband, Jonathan, this time. You see, although she still loved Terrence, she had decided to settle for watching him interact with their children, who looked so much like him, as they shared a wonderful, loving relationship. Angelica took pride in knowing that because of her loving Terrence so much, there were four children and in the future maybe more grands and many more great grands forth coming. After thinking about it, she had no regrets for tricking Terrence into the three of the most beautiful and most enjoyable sexual encounters that she could/would never forget. Although tricking Terrence might have been wrong by someone else's standards, it was a real blessing by Angelica's. She thought that the exchange for chasing after someone who wants someone else; then being able to see what was created from the chase was not a bad deal after all. At that moment Angelica looked at Terrence and thought, "But, if you, Mr. Terrence Watson ever want another "roll-in-the-hay, I will always be near to oblige you". When Terrence looked up and saw that lustful, come-hither look in her eyes that he had learned in the past to run from, he immediately turned his head. Angelica then thought, "Oh well, maybe not yet, but who knows, maybe next month at, Our family Thing To Do or some other month during Our Vacation Time Together. She then sat back in her chair and smiled, looking at Terrence and then at the children that had come forth from her getting what she wanted when she wanted it, no matter what the costs!!